100 Reasons to Celebrate

We invite you to join us in celebrating
Mills & Boon's centenary. Gerald Mills and
Charles Boon founded Mills & Boon Limited
in 1908 and opened offices in London's Covent
Garden. Since then, Mills & Boon has become
a hallmark for romantic fiction, recognised
around the world.

We're proud of our 100 years of publishing
excellence, which wouldn't have been achieved
without the loyalty and enthusiasm of our
authors and readers.

Thank you!

Each month throughout the year there will
be something new and exciting to mark the
centenary, so watch for your favourite authors,
captivating new stories, special limited
edition collections…and more!

Dear Reader

I'm a passionate reader of Mills & Boon novels, and the magic of creating exciting stories for the world's most well-known publisher of romance will never fade. I have always adored happy endings.

What a wonderful achievement it is that Mills & Boon is celebrating its 100th birthday in 2008! Could there be any better testament to the enduring power of romance? I'm thrilled to be a part of those celebrations.

Let me tell you something about this story. My hero, Leonidas, was born in my imagination when he swaggered with sarcasm through Rashad and Tilda's story, THE DESERT SHEIKH'S CAPTIVE WIFE.

Leonidas has a big personality, and he needed a strong lady to match him. Maribel wants the very best for her son, Elias, and she is ready to fight for what she believes is right. How she brings Leonidas round to her point of view makes for entertaining reading.

With best wishes

Lynne Graham

THE GREEK TYCOON'S DEFIANT BRIDE

BY
LYNNE GRAHAM

⊙™ MILLS & BOON®
Pure reading pleasure

First published in Great Britain 2007
Harlequin Mills & Boon Limited,
Eton House, 18-24 Paradise Road, Richmond, Surrey TW9 1SR

© Lynne Graham 2007

ISBN: 978 0 263 86400 7

Set in Times Roman 10½ on 12¼ pt
01-0208-49877

Printed and bound in Spain
by Litografia Rosés, S.A., Barcelona

THE RICH, THE RUTHLESS AND THE REALLY HANDSOME

How far will they go to win their wives?

A trilogy by Lynne Graham

Three men blessed with power, wealth and looks—
what more can they need? Wives, that's what…
and they'll use whatever means to take them!

Prince Rashad of Bakhar, heir to a desert kingdom,
Leonidas Pallis, scion of one of Greece's leading
dynasties, and Sergio Torrente, an impossibly
charismatic, self-made Italian billionaire. They were
best friends when they studied at Oxford and learnt
that it was better *never* to fall in love. Now, led by
passion, Rashad, Leonidas and Sergio have finally
found the women they want to marry and will use their
influence, pay their money, but keep their emotions
firmly under wraps to get what they want. Only none
has bargained on being brought to his knees by his
chosen wife… Or having his cold heart melted!

Coming in April:

Sergio's story!

CHAPTER ONE

WHEN the limousine appeared, a perceptible wave of anticipation rippled through the well-dressed cliques of people gathered on the church steps. Two cars had already drawn up in an advance guard, from which muscular men wearing dark glasses and talking into walkie-talkies had emerged to fan out in a protective cordon. At a signal from the security team the chauffeur finally approached the passenger door of the limo. The buzz in the air intensified, heads craning for a better view, eyes avid with curiosity.

Leonidas Pallis stepped out onto the pavement and immediately commanded universal attention. A Greek tycoon to his polished fingertips, he stood six feet three inches tall. A staggeringly handsome man, he wore a black cashmere overcoat and a designer suit with an elegance that was lethally sexy. That cutting-edge sophistication, however, was matched by a cold-blooded reserve and ruthlessness that made people very nervous. Born into one of the richest families in the world and to parents whose decadence was legendary, Leonidas had established a wild reputation at an early age. But no Pallis in living memory had displayed his extraordinary brilliance in business. A billionaire many times over, he was the golden idol of the Pallis clan and as much feared as he was fêted.

Everyone had wondered if he would bother to attend the memorial service. After all, just over two years had passed since Imogen Stratton had died in a drug-fuelled car crash. Although she had not been involved with Leonidas at the time, she had enjoyed an on-off association with him since he'd been at university. Imogen's mother, Hermione, swam forward to greet her most important guest with gushing satisfaction, for the presence of Leonidas Pallis turned the event into a social occasion worthy of comment. But the Greek billionaire cut the social pleasantries to a minimum—the Strattons were virtual strangers. While Imogen was alive he had neither met them nor wished to meet them and he did not have an appetite for fawning flattery.

Ironically the one person he had expected to greet him at the church, his only surviving acquaintance in the Stratton family circle, had yet to show her face: Imogen's cousin, Maribel Greenaway. Refusing an invitation to join the front pew line-up, Leonidas chose a much less prominent seat and sank down into it with the fluid grace of a panther. As quickly, he wondered why he had come when Imogen had despised such conventions. She had revelled in her fame as a fashion model and party girl. Living to be noticed and admired, Imogen had loved to shock even more. Yet she had worked hard at pleasing him until her absorption in drugs had concluded his interest in her. His hard-sculpted mouth flattened. Ultimately, he had cut her out of his life. Attending her funeral had presented a challenge and the fallout from that rare inner conflict had been explosive. The past was past, however, and like regret, not a place Leonidas had ever been known to visit.

* * *

Maribel nosed her elderly car into the parking space. She was horribly late and in a fierce hurry. At speed she re-angled the driving mirror and, with a brush in one hand and a clip gripped between her teeth, attempted to put her hair up. Newly washed and still damp, the shoulder-length fall of chestnut was rebellious. When the clip broke between her impatient fingers she could've wept with frustration. Throwing the brush aside, she smoothed her hair down with frantic fingers while simultaneously attempting to get out of the car. From the minute she'd got up that morning everything had gone wrong. Or perhaps the endless line of mini-disasters had begun the night before, when her aunt Hermione had phoned to say dulcetly that she would quite understand if Maribel found it too diffi-cult to attend the memorial service.

Maribel had winced, gritted her teeth at that news and said nothing. Over the past eighteen months her relatives had made it clear that she was now *persona non grata* as far as they were concerned. That had hurt, since Maribel cherished what family connections she had left. Even so, she fully understood their reservations. Not only had she never fitted the Stratton family mould, but she had also broken the rules of acceptance.

Her aunt and uncle set great store on looks, money and social status. Appearances were hugely important to them. Nevertheless, when Maribel had been orphaned, her mother's brother had immediately offered his eleven-year-old niece a home with his own three children. In the image-conscious Stratton household Maribel had had to learn how to melt into the background, where her failings in the beauty, size and grace stakes would awaken less censure and irritation. Those years would have been bleak, had they not been enlivened by Imogen's effervescent sense of fun. Although Imogen and Maribel had had not the slightest thing in common, Maribel had become deeply attached to the cousin who was three years her senior.

That was the main reason why Maribel was determined that nothing should be allowed to interfere with her sincere need to attend the service and pay her last respects. *Nothing,* she reminded herself doggedly, not even a powerful level of personal discomfiture. That sense of unease exasperated her. Over two years had gone by. She had no business still being so sensitive—*he* didn't have a sensitive bone in his body.

Her violet-blue eyes took on a militant sparkle and her chin came up. She was twenty-seven years old. She had a doctorate and she was a university tutor in the ancient history department of the university. She was intelligent, level-headed and practical. She liked men as friends or colleagues, but had reached the conclusion that they were far too much hassle in any closer capacity. After the appalling upheaval and the grieving process that she had had to work through in the wake of Imogen's sudden death, Maribel had finally found contentment. She liked her life. She liked her life very much. Why should she even care about what *he* might think? He had probably never thought about her again.

In that mood, she mounted the church steps and took the first available seat near the back of the nave. She focused on the service, looking neither right nor left while her sixth sense fingered down her taut spine and her skin prickled. Self-conscious pink began to blossom in her cheeks. *He* was present. She knew he was present and didn't know how. When she couldn't withstand temptation any longer, she glanced up and saw him several rows ahead on the other side of the aisle. The Pallis height and build were unmistakable, as was the angle of his arrogant dark head and the fact that at least three extremely attractive females had contrived to seat themselves within easy reach of him. Involuntarily she was amused. Had Leonidas been a rare animal, he would long ago have been hunted to extinction. As it was, he was dazzlingly handsome, totally untamed and a notorious womaniser. He mesmerised her sex into bad behaviour. No doubt the women hovering near him now would attempt to chat him up before the end of the service.

Without warning, Leonidas turned his head and surveyed her, the onslaught of his brilliant dark deep-set eyes striking her much like a bullet suddenly slamming into tender flesh. Her fight-or-flight response went into overdrive. Caught unawares and looking when she would have given almost anything to appear totally impervious to his existence, Maribel froze. Like a fish snared by a hook and left dangling, she felt horribly trapped. Mustering her self-discipline and her manners, she managed to give him a slight wooden nod of polite acknowledgement and returned her attention to the order of service in her hands. The booklet trembled in her grasp. She breathed in slow and deep and steadied her hold, fighting the riptide of memory threatening to blow a dangerous hole in her defences.

The glamorous blonde who slid into the pew beside her provided a welcome diversion. Hanna had belonged to the same modelling agency as Imogen. Indifferent to the fact that the vicar was speaking, Hanna lamented at length about the traffic that had led to her late arrival and then took out a mirror to twitch her hair into place.

'Will you introduce me to Leonidas Pallis?' Hanna stage-whispered as she renewed her lip gloss. 'I mean, you've known him for ever.'

Maribel continued to focus her attention on the service. She could not credit that once again a woman was trying to use her to get to Leonidas and she was quick to dismiss the idea that she could ever have been deemed an acquaintance of his. 'But not in the way you mean.'

'Yeah, you were like living as Imogen's housekeeper or whatever in those days, but he must still remember you. Have you any idea how rare that is? Very few people can claim *any* sort of a connection with Leonidas Pallis!'

Maribel said nothing. Her throat felt as if a lump of hysteria were wedged at the foot of it and she was not the sort of woman who threw hysterical fits. It was ironic that she could only think about Imogen, who had set her heart on a man she could not have, a man who would never care enough to give her the stability she had so desperately needed. Sometimes it had been very hard for Maribel to mind her own business while she had lived on the sidelines of her cousin's life, forced to witness her every mistake. The discovery that she herself was equally capable of blind stupidity had been hugely humiliating and not a lesson she was likely to forget in a hurry.

Hanna was impervious to the hint that silence might be welcome, adding, 'I just thought that if you introduced me, it would look more casual and less staged.'

Casual? Hanna was wearing a candy-pink suit so tight and so short she could barely sit in it. The feathery hat-confection in her long, streaming blonde hair was overkill and would have been more appropriate at a wedding.

'Please…please…please. He is so absolutely delicious in the flesh,' the other woman crooned pleadingly in Maribel's ear.

And a total, absolute bastard, Maribel reflected helplessly, only to be very much shocked by such a thought occurring to her in church and on such a serious occasion. Face colouring with shame, she cleansed her mind of that angry, bitter thought.

Leonidas had decided to be amused by that stony little nod from Maribel. The only woman he had ever met who refused to be impressed by him. A challenge he had been unable to resist, he acknowledged. His heavily lidded dark gaze roamed at an indolent pace over her, noting the changes with earthy masculine appreciation. Maribel had slimmed down, the better to show off the abundant swell of her full breasts and the voluptuous curve of her hips. The spring sunlight arrowing though a stained glass window far above glinted over hair the colour of maple syrup, skin like clotted cream and a generous mouth. Not beautiful, not even pretty, yet for some reason she had always contrived to grab his attention. Only this time he believed that he could finally understand why he was looking: she had the vibrant, sensual glow of a sun-ripened peach. He wondered if he was responsible for awakening that feminine awareness. Just as quickly, he wondered if he could seduce her into a repeat performance. And, on that one lingering look and that one manipulative thought, his slumbering libido roused to volcanic strength and sharpened his interest.

* * *

As the service drew to a close Maribel was keen to melt back out of the church in a departure as quiet as her arrival. That urge intensified when she noted the immediate surge up the aisle by her aunt and cousins, who were clearly determined to intercept Leonidas before he could leave. Unfortunately, Maribel's passage was blocked by Hanna.

'Why are you in such a hurry?' Hanna hissed, when Maribel attempted to ease past her stationary figure. 'Leonidas was looking in this direction. He's already noticed me. I asked you for such a tiny favour.'

'Someone as beautiful as you doesn't need an introduction,' Maribel whispered in sheer desperation.

Hanna laughed and preened. With a toss of her rippling golden tresses, she sashayed out into the aisle like a guided missile ready to lock onto a target. Several inches shorter, Maribel used the blonde as cover and ducked out in her wake to speed for the exit like a lemming rushing at a cliff. It wasn't cool to be so keen to avoid Leonidas, but so what? Mindful of the reality that her aunt no longer wished to acknowledge her as a member of the family, Maribel knew that it was her duty to embrace a low profile. In her haste, however, she cannoned into the photographer lying in wait beyond the doors. Wondering why she was spluttering an apology when the man was assailing her with furious abuse, Maribel rubbed the shoulder that had been bruised by the collision and hurried on out and back to the car park.

Unreceptive to the many opposing attempts to gain his attention, Leonidas strode out to the church porch. He was thoroughly intrigued by the mode and speed of his quarry's flight, because Maribel was, as a rule, wonderfully well

mannered and conservative. He had expected her to hover
unwillingly out of politeness and speak to him. But she had
not even paused to converse with the Strattons. While his
protection team prevented the lurking paparazzo from
snatching a photo of him, he watched Maribel approaching a little red car. For a small woman, she moved fast.
Lazily, he wondered if she was the only female who had
ever run away from him. Exasperated, he inclined his
handsome dark head to summon Vasos, his head of
security, to his side and gave him a concise command.

As Hermione Stratton, closely followed by her two
daughters, surged to a breathless halt by his side, Leonidas
spoke conventional words of regret before murmuring in
his dark, deep voice, 'Why did Maribel rush off?'

'Maribel?' The older woman opened her eyes very wide
and repeated the name as if she had never heard of her
niece.

'Probably racing home to that baby of hers,' the tallest,
blondest daughter opined with more than a touch of derision.

Although not an ounce of his surprise showed on his
lean bronzed features, Leonidas was stunned by that
careless statement. Maribel had a baby? *A baby?* Since
when? And by whom?

Hermione Stratton pursed her mouth into a little *moue*
of well-bred distaste. 'I'm afraid that she's a single parent.'

'And not in the fashionable category. She was left in the
lurch,' her daughter chipped in, smiling brightly at
Leonidas.

'Typical,' her sister giggled, rolling inviting big blue
eyes up at him. 'Even with all those brains, Maribel still
made the biggest mistake in the book!'

* * *

Five minutes after leaving the church, Maribel pulled off the road again to shed her black knitted jacket because she was overheating like mad. An attack of nerves always made her hot. Inside her head was an uninvited image of how Leonidas had looked in church. Breathtakingly beautiful. What else had she expected? He was still only thirty-one years old. Her hands clenched round the steering wheel. For a tiny moment, while she allowed her emotions to gain the upper hand, her knuckles showed white. Then slowly, deliberately, she relaxed her grip. She refused to concede that she had experienced any kind of emotional reaction and concentrated instead on being thoroughly irritated by her foolish and trite reflection regarding Leonidas' good looks. After all, shouldn't she have moved far beyond such juvenile ruminations by now?

Her rebellious mind served up painful memories and she gritted her teeth and literally kicked those thoughts back out of her head again. She slammed shut the equivalent of a mental steel door on recollections that would only stir up the feelings she was determined to keep buried. Clasping her seat belt again, she drove off to pick up her son.

Ginny Bell, her friend and childminder, lived in a cottage only a field away from Maribel's home. The older woman was a widow and a former teacher currently studying part-time for a master's degree. Slim and in her forties, with her black hair in a bob, she glanced up in surprise when Maribel appeared at her back door. 'My goodness, I wasn't expecting you back so soon!'

Elias abandoned his puzzle and hurtled across the kitchen to greet his mother. He was sixteen months old, an enchanting toddler with curly black hair and tobacco brown eyes. All the natural warmth and energy of his temperament shone in his smile and the exuberance with which he returned his mother's hug. Maribel drank in the familiar baby scent of his skin and was engulfed by a giant wave of love. Only after Elias's birth had she truly understood the intensity of a mother's attachment to her child. She had revelled in the year of maternity leave she'd taken to be with her baby. Returning to work even on a part-time basis had been a real challenge for her, and now she was never away from Elias for longer than a couple of hours without eagerly looking forward to the moment when she would get back to him again. Without even trying, Elias had become the very centre of her world.

Still puzzled by Maribel's swift return, Ginny was frowning. 'I thought your aunt and uncle were hosting a fancy buffet lunch after the service.'

Maribel briefly shared the content of her aunt's phone call the night before.

'My goodness, how can Hermione Stratton exclude you like that?' Ginny exclaimed, angrily defensive on the younger woman's behalf because, as a long-standing friend, she knew how much the Strattons owed to Maribel, who had loyally watched over Imogen while the model's family had given their daughter and her increasingly erratic and embarrassing behaviour a wide berth.

'Well, I blotted my copybook by having Elias and I can't say that I wasn't warned about how it would be,' Maribel countered with wry acceptance.

'When your aunt urged you to have a termination because she saw your pregnancy as a social embarrassment, she was going way beyond her remit. You had already told her that you wanted your baby and you're scarcely a feckless teenager,' Ginny reminded the younger woman with feeling. 'As for her suggestion that you wouldn't be able to cope, you're one of the most capable mothers I know!'

Maribel gave her a rueful look. 'I expect my aunt gave her advice in good faith. And to be fair—when Hermione was a girl it *was* a disgrace for a child to be born out of wedlock.'

'Why are you so magnanimous? That woman has always treated you like a Victorian poor relation!'

'It wasn't as bad as that. My aunt and uncle found it hard to understand my academic aspirations.' Maribel moved her hands in a dismissive gesture. 'I was the oddball of the family and just too different from my cousins.'

'They put a lot of pressure on you to conform.'

'But even more on Imogen,' Maribel declared, thinking of her fragile cousin, who had craved approval and admiration to such a degree that she had been able to handle neither rejection nor failure.

Elias squirmed to get down from his mother's lap so that he could investigate the arrival of the postman's van. He was a lively child with a mind that teemed with curiosity about the world that surrounded him. While Ginny went to the door to collect a parcel, Maribel gathered up all the paraphernalia that went with transporting a toddler between different houses.

'Can't you stay for coffee?' Ginny asked on her return.

'I'm sorry. I'd love to, but I've got loads of work to do.' But Maribel turned a slight guilty pink for she could have spared a half-hour. Unfortunately seeing Leonidas again had shaken her up and she craved the security of her own home. She scooped up Elias to take him out to her car, which was parked at the back door.

Her son was big for his age and lifting him was becoming more of an effort. She hefted him into his car seat. He put his own arms into the straps, displaying the marked streak of independence that sometimes put him at odds with his mother. 'Elias do,' he stated with purpose.

His bottom lip came out and he protested when she insisted on doing up the clasp on the safety belt. He wanted to do it himself, but she was determined not to give him the opportunity to master the technique of locking and releasing it. Having learnt to walk at an early age, Elias was already a skilled escape artist from chairs, buggies and play-pens.

Maribel drove back out onto the road and slowed down to overtake a silver car parked by the side of it. It was a bad place to stop and she was surprised to see a vehicle there. A hundred yards further on, she turned into the sun-dappled rambling lane overhung by trees that led to what had once been her home with her parents. She had inherited the picturesque old farmhouse after her father died and it had been rented out for many years. When the property had finally fallen vacant, everybody had expected her to sell up and plunge the proceeds into a trendy urban apartment. The discovery around the same time that she was pregnant, however, had turned Maribel's life upside down. After she had revisited the house where she had all too briefly enjoyed a wealth of parental love and attention, she had begun to appreciate that bringing up a child alone was going to demand a major change of focus and pace from her. She would have to give up her workaholic ways and make space in her busy schedule for a baby's needs.

Ignoring the comments about how old-fashioned and

isolated the property was, she had quietly got on with organising the refurbishment of the interior. Situated in a secluded valley and convenient to both London and Oxford, the farmhouse, she felt, offered her the best of both worlds. The convenience of having a good friend like Ginny living nearby had been the icing on the cake, even before Ginny had suggested that she take care of Elias while Maribel was at work.

'Mouse…Mouse…Mouse!' Elias chanted, wriggling like an eel and pushing at the door as Maribel unlocked it.

An extremely timid Irish wolfhound, Mouse was hiding under the table as usual. He would not emerge until he was reassured that it was only Maribel and Elias coming home. Struggling out from below the table because he was a very large dog, Mouse then welcomed his family with boisterous enthusiasm. Boy and dog rolled on the floor in a tumbling heap. Elias scrambled up. 'Mouse…up!' he instructed, to the manner born.

For a split-second, a flash of memory froze Maribel to the spot: Leonidas seven years earlier, asking when she planned on picking up the shirts lying on the floor. There had been that same note of imperious command and expectation, but not the same successful result because, intimidating though Leonidas was, Maribel had never been as eager to please as Mouse. Another image swiftly followed: Leonidas so domestically challenged and so outraged by the suggestion that he was helpless without servants that he had put an electric kettle on the hob.

Her son's yelp of pain jerked Maribel out of her abstraction. Elias had stumbled and bumped his head on the fridge. Tiredness made him clumsy. Maribel lifted him and rubbed his head in sympathy. Tear-drenched, furious brown eyes met hers, for the reverse side of his warmth and energy was a strong will and a temper of volcanic strength and durability. 'I know, I know,' she whispered gently, rocking him until his annoyance ebbed and his impossibly long black lashes began to droop.

She took him upstairs to the bright and cheerful nursery she had decorated with painstaking care and enjoyment. Removing his shoes and jacket, she settled him down in his cot with soothing murmurs. He went out like a light, yet she knew he wouldn't stay horizontal for very long. In sleep, he looked angelic and peaceful, but awake he could lay claim to neither trait. She watched him for a couple of minutes, involuntarily drawn into tracing the physical likeness that could only strike her with powerful effect on the same day that she had seen his father again. She wondered if her son was the only decent thing that Leonidas Pallis had ever created. It was a fight to get a grip on her thoughts again.

Accompanied by Mouse, Maribel went into the small sunlit room she used as a study and got straight down to marking the pile of essays awaiting her attention. Some time later, Mouse barked and nudged at her arm with an anxious whine. Ten seconds after that warning, she heard the approach of a car and she pushed back her chair. She was walking into the hall when she registered that other vehicles appeared to be arriving at the same time. Her brow furrowed in bewilderment, for she received few visitors and never in car loads.

Glancing out of the window, she stilled in consternation, for a long gleaming limousine now obscured her view of the garden and the field beyond it. Who else could it be but Leonidas Pallis? Her paralysis lasted for only a moment before she raced into the lounge, gathered up the toys lying on the rug and threw them into the toy box, which she thrust at frantic speed behind the sofa. The bell went even before she straightened from that task. She caught a glimpse of herself in the mirror: her blue eyes were wide with fear, and her face was pale as death. She rubbed her cheeks to restore some natural colour while apprehension made her mind race. What the heck was Leonidas doing here? How could he possibly have found out where she lived? And why should he have even wanted to know? The bell rang again in a shrill, menacing burst. She recalled the Pallis impatience all too well.

A dark sense of foreboding nudging at her, Maribel opened the door.

'Surprise…surprise,' Leonidas drawled softly.

Unnerved by the sheer smoothness of that greeting, Maribel froze and Leonidas took immediate advantage by stepping over the threshold. Her hand fell from the door as she turned to face him. After what had been a mere stolen glimpse in church, she got her first good look at him. His suit and coat were exquisitely tailored, designer-cut and worn with supreme *élan*. His height and breadth alone were intimidating, but for a woman his lean sculpted bone structure and utterly gorgeous dark, deep-set eyes had the biggest impact. Nor was that effect the least diminished by the fact that those ebony eyes were as dangerously direct and cutting as a laser beam. A tiny pulse began beating horribly fast at the foot of her throat, interfering with her ability to breathe.

'So what ever did happen to breakfast?' Leonidas murmured with honeyed derision.

A crimson tide of colour washed away Maribel's pallor

in a contrast as strong as blood on snow. Shock reverber-
ated through her as he punched an unapologetic hole
through the mind-block she had imposed on her memories
of that night after Imogen's funeral, just over two years
earlier. Flinching, she tore her gaze from his, hot with shame
and taut with disbelief that he should have dared to throw
that crack at her in virtually the first sentence he spoke. But
then what did Leonidas not dare? The last time she had met
his gaze, they had been a good deal closer and he had shaken
her awake to murmur with quite shattering cool and
command, 'Make me breakfast while I'm in the shower.'

In remembrance, a wave of dizziness washed over her
and her tummy flipped as though she had gone down too
fast in a lift. She would have done just about anything to
avoid the recollection of his cruel amusement that morning.
She had been gone by the time he'd emerged from that
shower. She had buried her mistake as deep as she could,
confiding in nobody, indeed resolving to take that particular secret to the grave with her. She was ashamed of the
events of that night and all too well aware that Leonidas
had not even a passing acquaintance with sensations like
shame or discomfiture. She was dismayed by the discovery that, even after two years, her defences were still laugh-
ably thin. So thin that he could still hurt her, she registered
in dismay.

'I would sooner not discuss that,' Maribel enunciated
with a wooden lack of expression.

Exasperated by that prissy response, Leonidas snapped
the front door shut with an authoritative hand and strolled
into the front room. Her taste had not changed, he noted.
Had he been presented with pictures of house interiors he
could easily have picked out hers. The room was full of

plants, towering piles of books and faded floral fabrics. Nothing seemed to match and yet there was a surprising stylishness and comfort to the effect she had achieved.

'Or why you bolted from the church today?' Leonidas queried, his rich, dark, accented drawl smooth as silk, but infinitely more disturbing.

Feeling trapped but determined not to overreact, Maribel studied his elegant grey silk tie. 'I wasn't bolting—I was simply in a hurry.'

'But how unlike you to disregard the social rituals of the occasion,' Leonidas censured softly. 'Yet another unusual experience for me. You are the only woman who runs away from me.'

'Maybe I know you better than the others do.' Maribel could have clapped her hand to her mouth in horror after that verbal reprisal simply tripped off her tongue without her even being aware that it was there. She was furious with herself, for in one foolish little sentence she had betrayed the fear, the anger, the bitterness and the loathing that she would have very much preferred to keep hidden from him.

CHAPTER TWO

LEONIDAS was not amused by that retaliation. The devil that lurked never far below his polished granite surface leapt out. While women of all ages fawned on him and hung on his every word, Maribel, it seemed, still favoured the acerbic response. He had never forgotten the one surprisingly sweet night when Maribel had used honey rather than vinegar in her approach. He had liked that; he had hugely preferred that different attitude, since he had neither taste nor tolerance for censure.

His brilliant eyes gleamed in liquid-gold warning below his luxuriant black lashes. 'Maybe you do,' Leonidas acknowledged without any inflection at all.

For a long, wordless moment, Leonidas took his fill while he looked at her, his gaze roaming over her with a boldness that came as naturally to him as aggression. His attention lingered on her strained violet-blue eyes, dropped to the luscious fullness of her mouth as it pouted against her peach-soft skin, and finally wandered lower to scan the full glory of her hourglass curves. It was a novelty to know that, this time around, she would most probably slap him if he touched her. After all, it wouldn't be the first time.

He almost smiled at the memory: his very first and still quite unique experience of female rejection.

Madly aware of that unashamedly sexual appraisal and unable to bear it any longer, Maribel flushed to her hairline and breathed curtly, 'Stop it!'

'Stop what? 'Leonidas growled, strong arousal now tugging at him, in spite of the powerful sense of intuition that warned him that there was something wrong. Even as he glanced back at her face, he picked up on her fear and wondered why she was scared. She had never been scared around him before, or so reluctant to meet his gaze. A faint sense of disappointment touched him, even while he wondered what was wrong with her.

'Looking at me like that!' For the first time in two long years, Maribel was hugely conscious of her body and she was furious that she could still be so easily affected by him.

Leonidas loosed an earthy masculine laugh. 'It's natural for me to look.'

Her slim hands coiled into fists of restraint. 'I don't like it.'

'Tough. Aren't you going to offer me coffee? Ask me to take off my coat and sit down?' Leonidas chided.

Maribel felt like a bird being played with by a cat and she snatched in a fractured breath. 'No.'

'What *has* happened to your manners?' Unasked, Leonidas peeled off his coat in a slow graceful movement that was curiously sexy and attracted her unwilling attention.

Maribel dragged her guilty eyes off him again, gritting her teeth, literally praying for self-discipline. He came between her and her wits. He brought sex into everything. He made her think and feel things that were not her choice. No matter how hard she fought it, there was a shameful hum of physical awareness travelling through her resisting body. He had always had that effect on her, *always*. Leonidas had provoked a sense of guilt in Maribel almost from the first moment of their meeting.

In a fluid stride, Leonidas closed the distance between them and lifted a hand to push up her chin and enforce the eye contact she was so keen to avoid. 'Was it the service? Did it upset you?'

He was now so close that Maribel trembled. She was taken aback by the ease with which he had touched her. She did not want to recall the fleeting intimacy that had broken down all normal barriers. She did not want to be reminded of the taste of his mouth or the evocative scent of his skin. 'No…it was good to remember her,' she said gruffly.

'Then what's the problem?' Mesmeric dark golden eyes assailed hers, powered by a larger-than-life personality that few could have withstood.

Her throat ached with her tension. 'There isn't one,' she told him unevenly. 'I just wasn't expecting you to call.'

'I'm usually a welcome visitor,' Leonidas murmured lazily, his relaxed rejoinder quite out of step with the keen penetration of his gaze.

As Maribel strove to keep a calm expression on her oval face her teeth chattered together behind her sealed lips for a split-second before she overcame that urge. 'Naturally I'm surprised to see you here. It's been a long time and I've moved house,' she pointed out, struggling to behave normally and say normal things. 'Did my aunt give you my address?'

'No. I had you followed.'

Maribel turned pale at that unnervingly casual admission. 'My goodness, why did you do that?'

'Curiosity? A dislike of relying on strangers for information?' Leonidas shrugged with languid cool. An infinitesimal movement out of the corner of his eye turned his attention below the table where a shaggy grey dog was endeavouring to curl its enormous body into the smallest possible space in the farthest corner. 'Theos...I did not even realise there was an animal here. What is the matter with it?'

Maribel seized on the distraction of Mouse's odd behaviour with enthusiasm. 'He's terrified of strangers and when he hides his head like that he seems to think he's invisible, so don't let on otherwise. Friendly overtures frighten him.'

'Still collecting lame ducks?' Leonidas quipped and, as he turned his head away, he caught a glimpse through the window of a hen pecking in the flower bed at the front of the house. 'You keep poultry here?'

His intonation was that of a jet-setter aghast at her deeply rural lifestyle. Maribel was willing to bet that Leonidas had never before been so close to domestic fowl, and in another mood she would have laughed at his expression and rattled on the window to chase the hen away from her plants. Unable to relax, she resolved to treat him as she would have treated any other unexpected visitor. 'Look, I'll make some coffee,' she proffered, thrusting open the kitchen door.

'I'm not thirsty. Tell me what you've been doing over the past couple of years,' he invited softly.

A chill ran down her taut spinal cord before she turned back to him. He couldn't know about Elias, she reasoned inwardly. Why should he even suspect? Unless someone had said something at the service? But why the heck should anyone have mentioned her or her child? As far as her relatives were concerned she was a geek who led a deeply boring life. Scolding herself for the unfamiliar paranoia that was ready to pounce and take hold of her, Maribel tilted her chin. 'I've been turning this place into a habitable home. It needed a lot of work. That kept me busy.'

Leonidas watched her hands lace together in a restive motion and untangle again. She folded her arms and shifted position in a revealing display of anxiety that any skilled observer would have recognised. 'I believe you have a child now,' he delivered smooth as glass, and all the time as his own tension rose he was telling himself that he had to be wrong, his suspicions ridiculously fanciful.

'Yes—yes, I have. I didn't think you'd be too interested in that piece of news,' Maribel countered in a determined recovery, forcing a wry smile onto her taut lips, while wondering how on earth he had found out that she had become a mother. 'As I recall it, you used to give friends with kids the go-by.'

Leonidas would have been the first to admit that that was true: he had never had any interest in children and found the doting fondness of parents for their offspring a bore and an irritation. Nobody acquainted with him would have dreamt of wheeling out their progeny for him to admire.

'Who told you I'd had a child?' Maribel enquired a shade tightly.

'The Strattons.'

'I'm surprised it was mentioned.' While fighting to keep her voice light, Maribel was wondering frantically what she would say if he asked her what age her child was.

Would she lie? *Could* she lie on such a subject? She was in a situation that she would have done almost anything to avoid. She did not believe that she could lie about such a serious matter and still live with her conscience. 'Was it the "left-in-the-lurch" version?' she asked.

A rare smile of amusement slashed the Greek tycoon's beautifully shaped mouth. 'Yes.'

'That's not how it was,' Maribel declared, attempting not to stare, because when he smiled the chill factor vanished from his lean, hard-boned features and banished the forbidding dark reserve that put people so much on their guard.

Without warning, distaste that she had slept with another man assailed Leonidas and killed his momentary amusement on the subject. He marvelled at that stab of possessiveness that ran contrary to his nature. His affairs were always casual, hampered by neither emotion nor sentimentality. But then, he had known Maribel for a long time and he had become her first lover. Perhaps that had been inevitable, he reasoned, still in search of the precise trigger that had fired him into making that discovery, more than two years earlier. Once he had discovered how she felt about him, the awareness had lent a strangely enjoyable intimacy to their encounters.

'How was it?' he heard himself ask, and it was the sort of question he never asked, but he was determined to satisfy his curiosity.

Maribel was disconcerted by that enquiry and she spread her hands in a jerky motion. Her tension was climbing steadily. 'It wasn't complex. I found myself pregnant and I wanted the baby.'

Leonidas wondered at her wording. Why no reference

to the father? Another one-night stand? Had he given her a taste for them? Had he ever really known her? He would have sworn that Maribel Greenaway was one of the last women alive likely to embrace either promiscuity or unmarried motherhood. Her outlook on life was conservative. She went to church; she volunteered for charity work. She wore unrevealing clothes. A frown line dividing his sleek ebony brows, his gaze skimmed over the view through the kitchen doorway. There, however, his attention screeched to an abrupt halt and doubled back to re-examine the brightly coloured, magnetised alphabet letters adorning the refrigerator door. Those letters spelled out a familiar name. A powerful sense of disbelief gripped him.

'What do you call your child?' Leonidas murmured thickly.

Maribel went rigid. 'Why are you asking me that?'

'And why are you avoiding answering me?' Leonidas shot back at her.

A horrible cold knot twisted tight inside her stomach. It was not something she could hide, not something she could lie about, for her child's name was a matter of public record. 'Elias,' she almost whispered, her voice dying on her at the worst possible moment.

It was the name of his grandfather and also one of his, and she pronounced it correctly in the Greek fashion, El-lee-us, not as someone English might have said it. Leonidas was so much shocked by that awareness that he was struck dumb, as he could not initially accept that what had only been the mildest of craziest suspicions might actually turn out to be true.

'I always liked the name,' Maribel told him in a last-ditch attempt at a cover-up.

'Elias is a Pallis name. My grandfather had it and so also do I.' Hard dark eyes rested on her with cold intensity. 'Why did you choose to use it?'

Maribel felt as though an icy hand were closing round her vocal cords and chest and making it impossible for her to breathe properly. 'Because I liked it,' she said again, because she could think of nothing else to say.

Leonidas swung away from her, lean brown hands clenching into fists of frustration. He had no time for mysteries or games that were not of his own making. His chequered life had taught him many things, but patience was not one of them. He refused to believe what his brain was striving to tell him. He did not do unprotected sex. A risk-taker in business and sport and equally fearless in many other fields, he was cautious when it came to contraception, always choosing the safe approach. He did not want children. He had never wanted children. Even less had he ever wished to run the risk of giving some woman a literal gun to hold to his head and his wallet. For what else could an unplanned child be to a man of his extreme wealth? A serious liability and a complication he could do without. It was a mistake he had always thought he was too smart to make. But he was well aware that the night after Imogen's funeral he had been in a very bizarre mood and he had abandoned his usual caution. More than once.

Maribel surveyed Leonidas with a surge of reluctant perception. Severe tension held his lean, powerful body taut. He was staggered and he was appalled, and she quite understood that. She did not blame him for his carelessness in getting her pregnant. It was true that she had felt rather differently when she had first discovered her condition, but the passage of time had altered her perspective.

After all, Elias had enriched her life to an almost inde-scribable degree and she could hardly regret his concep-tion.

'Let's not discuss this,' she murmured gently.

That suggestion outraged Leonidas. How could a woman with her extraordinary intellect say something so foolish? But was it possible that she could have given birth to his child without even letting him know that she was pregnant? Surely it had to be impossible? His logic refused to accept her in such a role—she was a very conventional woman. Yet why else had she named her child Elias? Why was she so nervous? Why was she irrationally trying to evade even discussing the matter?

'Is the child mine?' Leonidas demanded harshly.

Her natural colour had ebbed and with it the strength of her voice. 'He's mine. I see no reason to add anything else to that statement.'

'Don't be stupid. I asked a straight question and I will have a straight answer. What age is he?'

'I'm not prepared to discuss Elias with you.' Dry-mouthed, her heart beating so fast she felt nauseous, Maribel straightened her spine. 'We have nothing to talk about. I'm sorry, but I would like you to leave.'

Leonidas could not give credence to what he was hearing. In all his life he had never been addressed in such a fashion. 'Are you out of your mind?' he breathed in a raw undertone. 'You think you can throw this bombshell at me and then tell me to go away?'

'I didn't throw anything at you. You reached your own conclusions without any assistance from me. I don't want to argue with you.' Her blue eyes were violet with a curious mix of defiance and entreaty.

'But if I hadn't reached the correct conclusion, you would surely have contradicted me,' Leonidas reasoned with harsh bite. 'As you did not, I can only assume that you believe Elias to be my child.'

'He is mine.' Maribel linked her hands tightly together to prevent them from trembling. 'I'm quite sure you don't want my advice, but I'll give it all the same. Please consider this issue in a calm and logical way first.'

'Calm? Logical?' Leonidas growled, affronted by that particular choice of words.

'Elias is healthy, happy and secure. He lacks nothing. There is no reason for you to be concerned or involved in any way in our lives,' Maribel told him tautly, willing him to listen, understand and accept those facts.

Rage was rising in Leonidas with a ferocity he had not experienced since his sister had died when he was sixteen. How dared she seek to exclude him from his child's life? Elias had to be *his* child, *his* son. Had it been otherwise, Maribel would have said so. But bewilderment held him back from the much more aggressive response ready to blast from him. Why was she trying to get rid of him if Elias was his child? What kind of sense did that make?

'Did you assume I wouldn't want to know? Is that what lies at the foot of this nonsense?' Dark eyes shimmering gold, Leonidas studied her in wrathful challenge. 'Are you presuming to believe that you know how I would feel if I had a child? You do not know. Even I do not know when such news comes at me out of nowhere!'

The atmosphere was so hot and tense Maribel would not have been surprised to hear it sizzle and see it smoke.

'When was he born?' Leonidas demanded.

Her neck and her shoulders ached with the tension of her

rigid stance. All the legendary force of the Pallis will was trained on her in the onslaught of his fierce dark gaze. Never had she been more conscious of his strength of character and it occurred to her that parting with a few harmless facts might actually dampen down his animosity. She gave the date.

The silence seemed to last for ever. In the circumstances and with such a date, Leonidas knew immediately that there was virtually no chance that anyone else could have fathered her child. 'I want to see him.'

Maribel went white and shook her head in urgent negative, chestnut brown hair flying round her cheeks in a glossy fall. 'No. I won't allow that.'

'You won't...*allow*...that?' Leonidas breathed in rampant disbelief.

Maribel wished that there had been a more diplomatic way of telling him that. Unhappily, she had no precedent to follow because people didn't say no to Leonidas Pallis. 'No' was not a word he was accustomed to hearing. 'No' was not a word he knew how to accept. From birth he had had every material thing he had ever wanted or asked for, while being starved of the much more important childhood needs. But he had survived by tuning out the emotional stuff, getting by without it. Now when he desired something, he simply went all out to take it and sensible people didn't get in his way. He was as ruthless as only a very powerful personality could be when he was crossed. She knew very well that her refusal struck him as a deeply offensive challenge and just how unfortunate that reality was.

'I won't allow it,' she whispered apologetically while she stood as straight and stiff as a statue, struggling not to feel intimidated.

But Leonidas was already striding past her to snatch up the photo frame on a corner table. 'Is this him?' he breathed in a thickened undertone, staring down with a strong air of bemusement at the snap of the smiling toddler clutching a toy lorry.

It was natural human curiosity, she told herself, fighting to control the sense of panic clawing at her. 'Yes,' she conceded in reluctant confirmation.

Leonidas scanned the photo with an intensity that would have stripped paint. He studied the little boy's olive skin and black curly hair and his dark-as-jet eyes. Although he could never recall looking at any other child with the slightest interest and had absolutely no basis for comparison, he thought that Elias was, without a shade of doubt, the most handsome baby he had ever seen. From his level eyebrows to his determined little chin, he just oozed strong Pallis genes.

'Please go, Leonidas,' Maribel urged tautly. 'Don't make this a battle between us. Elias is a happy child.'

'He is also self-evidently a Pallis,' Leonidas pronounced in a bemused tone, his Greek accent more marked than usual.

'No, he's a Greenaway.'

Lush black lashes swept up on sizzling dark golden eyes. 'Maribel...he is a Pallis. You cannot call a dog a cat just because you want to, and why should you want to?'

'I can think of many reasons. Now that you've forced me to satisfy your curiosity, will you leave?' Maribel was trembling. She was tempted to snatch that precious picture of her son from his lean brown hand. All her protective antenna were operating on high alert.

'Acquit me of a motive as superficial as that of mere

curiosity,' Leonidas censured. 'You owe me an explanation—'

'I owe you nothing and I want you to go.' Swallowing back the thick taste of panic in her throat, Maribel moved forward and snatched up the phone. 'If you don't leave right now, I'll call the police.'

Leonidas gave her a disconcerted glance and then threw back his handsome dark head and laughed out loud. 'Why would you do something so mad?'

'This is my home. I want you to leave.'

'In the same hour that I find out that you may be the mother of my only child?' Innate caution and shrewdness were already exercising restraint on Leonidas. He knew it would be most unwise to acknowledge Elias as his before stringent DNA testing had been carried out and the blood bond fully proven by scientific means. Yet he knew in his bones that Elias was his child. He did not know how he knew but he did, and he was already reaching the conclusion that the situation could have been a great deal worse. At least he had Maribel to deal with, and not some mercenary, calculating harpy without morals.

'I *will* call the police,' Maribel threatened unsteadily, terrified that Elias would waken and make some sound upstairs, and that Leonidas would immediately insist on going up to see him.

Leonidas slung her a confounded look and flung his arms wide in a gesture that was expansively Greek and impressive. 'What is the matter with you? Is this hysteria? Are you at risk of robbery or assault? Is that why you need to talk garbage about calling the police?'

Her eyes were as bright a purple-blue as wild violets, an impression heightened by her pallor and tension. 'I want you to forget you came here and forget what you think you may have found out. For all our sakes.'

'Is there some other guy hanging around who thinks that Elias is his child?' Leonidas enquired grimly, seizing on the only motive he could think of that might explain why she was so eager for him to stage a vanishing act.

A band of tension was starting to pound behind Maribel's smooth brow and tighten there like a painful vice. Standing up to Leonidas Pallis in such a mood was like being battered by a fierce storm. 'Of course not.' Distaste showed openly in her oval face. 'That's a really sleazy suggestion.'

'Women do stuff like that all the time,' Leonidas told her cynically, and he was not wholly convinced by her denial. Having watched Imogen manipulate Maribel, he had soon appreciated that, while Maribel might be exceptionally brainy, she could also be very gullible when her emotions were engaged. 'If that isn't the problem, spare me the theatrical speeches about forgetting I came here. How likely is that?'

'Just this once I'm asking you to think about someone other than yourself. If that's theatrical, I'm sorry, but that's how it is.' With an unsteady hand, Maribel pushed the hair back from her cheekbone.

Leonidas gave her a quelling look of granite hardness. 'I'm not listening to this claptrap. Where is Elias?'

Maribel stepped into the hall and yanked open the front door with a perspiring hand. 'I'll get the police, Leonidas. I mean it. I've got nothing to lose.'

'My business card. Call me when you come to your senses.' Leonidas settled a card down on the table.

'I won't be changing my mind any time soon,' Maribel declared defiantly.

Leonidas came to a halt in front of her. Dangerous dark golden eyes slammed down into hers. 'You want to start a war? You think you can handle that? You think you can handle me?' he growled. 'You could never handle me.'

'But I have to, because I will not accept you in any part of my son's life. I'll do whatever it takes to protect him from you!' Maribel swore in a feverish rush, determination etched into every rigid line of her small, shapely figure.

'Protect him from me? What are you trying to say? You become offensive and without reason.' Lean. dark features set with chilling intent, Leonidas shot her a forbidding appraisal. 'Why? I expected better from you. Is this some sort of payback, Maribel? Are you angry that it took me two years to look you up?'

Maribel wanted to kill him and it was not the first time he had filled her with so much rage and pain that she barely knew what she was thinking any more. Nobody could be more provocative than Leonidas Pallis. Nobody knew better how to put the metaphorical boot in and hurt. Sensible people did not make an enemy of him. But then a sensible woman, she thought in an agony of bitter self-loathing, would never have gone to bed with him in the first place.

'Why would I be?' Maribel murmured helplessly. 'I don't even like you.'

Virtually nothing shocked Leonidas as, while he'd been growing up, he had seen all the worst facets of human nature as paraded by his dysfunctional mother, but that declaration from Maribel shocked him. He had always viewed her no-nonsense front as a defensive shell. He regarded her as a caring, sympathetic woman with a genuine soft centre, sadly condemned to have her good nature taken advantage of by the users and abusers of the world. But in the space of half an hour, Maribel had turned everything he believed he knew about her upside down and gone out of her way to attack and insult him.

Yet, from what he could work out, she appeared to be the mother of his child. He wondered if stress was making her hysterical, if she just couldn't cope with the situation. He did not accept that she didn't like him. He knew she loved him and he had known that almost as long as he had known her. She was not a changeable woman. That she had given birth to his child, rather than choose to have a termination, struck him as perfectly understandable.

Lean, darkly handsome face bleak, Leonidas climbed into his limousine. A Pallis and an alpha male personality to the core of his aggressive being, he wasted no time in making his next move. Lifting the phone, he called the executive head of his international legal team and asked for a copy of Elias Greenaway's birth certificate to be obtained. He gave the details and ignored the staggered silence that fell at the other end of the line, because Leonidas Pallis never explained his actions to anyone, or laid out the full details of a situation unless he chose to do so.

'In the morning, I also want a full briefing with regard to my rights as a father in this country.'

Furiously angry and in fighting mode, Leonidas marvelled afresh at Maribel's offensive behaviour and unreasonable attitude. As he recalled her words his hostility grew ever stronger. To refuse him his natural desire to see the child! To suggest that the child should be protected from him and would be better off without him! His sense of honour was outraged by the shameful accusations she had dared to make.

And, all the while, he kept on seeing images of Maribel flashing him that defiant look, her luscious pink mouth taut with censure. His shimmering dark eyes scorched and hardened. How could she have had his baby without telling him? When the photo of the little boy came to mind, however, he tensed, for he preferred being angry with Maribel to thinking about the matter that lay at the heart of it all.

CHAPTER THREE

ELIAS was grizzling noisily for attention by the time that Maribel finally emerged from her overwrought stance behind the front door. The limousine, with its accompanying cavalcade, was long gone.

Recovering her wits, Maribel hastened upstairs and swept her son from his cot with an enthusiasm that made him laugh and shout with pleasure; there was nothing Elias loved more than good old-fashioned horseplay. Trembling, Maribel lifted him high and then hugged him tight, knowing that she would want to die if anything happened to him. She had done the right thing in sending Leonidas away; she *knew* she had done the right thing.

But what were the chances that Leonidas would stay away? Maribel looped her damp hair off her anxious brow. Leonidas, who was mentally primed only to do what he wanted to do, and likely to want to do what he was told he could not or should not do? Elias had the same bloody-minded competitive trait. Maybe it was a male thing. She took Elias out into the garden with Mouse. While her son and the wolfhound ran about doing nothing much that she could see but hugely enjoying themselves, Maribel sat on the swing and let her memory take her back seven years…

* * *

Imogen had bought a house in Oxford and had persuaded Maribel, who had then been a student, to move in and take care of the property for her. Maribel had been happy to reduce her expenses and take care of the domestic trivia that Imogen, who had often been away from home, couldn't be bothered with. Imogen had been twenty-three, and her career as a fashion model had failed to reach the dazzling heights she'd craved. An indomitable party girl, Imogen had wasted no time in introducing herself to Leonidas Pallis when she'd run into him at a nightclub. At the time Leonidas had been a student at Oxford University.

'He is so rich money means nothing to him. His party was *amazing!*' Imogen, a tall, strikingly lovely blonde in a trendy short dress, was so excited that her words were tripping over each other. 'He's an A-list celebrity and so cool, he just freaks me out. Oh, and did I mention what a total babe he is?'

Listening to that artless flood of confidence, Maribel was more worried than impressed, because Imogen was all too easily influenced by the wrong people. The advent of an infamous Greek playboy, who crashed cars and abseiled down skyscrapers for thrills, struck Maribel as very bad news. Dating the heir to the Pallis billions, however, very much enhanced Imogen's earning power as a model. Suddenly she was in great demand, rubbing shoulders with the rich and famous and flying round the world to shoots, weekend parties and endless vacations.

'He's the one…he's the *one*. I want to marry him and become a Greek tycoon's fabulously wealthy wife. I'll die if he dumps me!' Imogen gasped at the end of the first fort-night, and that same night she dragged Leonidas in to meet Maribel without the slightest warning.

Clad in tartan pyjamas, and curled up with a research

paper on carbon dating and a mug of hot cocoa clutched in her hand, Maribel was appalled when Imogen simply walked into her bedroom with Leonidas in tow.

'This is my cousin, Maribel, my best friend in the whole world,' Imogen declared. 'She's a student like you.'

Lounging in the doorway, Leonidas gave Maribel a lazy smile of amusement and the shock of his intense attraction hit Maribel like an electric charge. She didn't know where to look or how to handle it, since the even bigger shock was that she had the capacity to feel that way! Up until that point, Maribel's dating forays had been unenthusiastic and always disappointing. One guy had got friendly with her only to steal her work, and another had tried to get her to do his assignments for him. Then there were the many who expected sex on the first date and the others who drank themselves into a stupor. None of them had given her goose-bumps or, indeed, an instant of excitement—until Leonidas appeared on the horizon.

And Maribel being Maribel, she was sick with guilt at being attracted to her cousin's man. That very first night, she shut out that awareness and refused to allow herself to take it out again. In the month that followed, she barely saw Imogen, who stayed in Leonidas' properties in Oxford, London and abroad. And then, just as suddenly, the brief affair was over, just one more fling in Pallis terms, but it had meant a great deal more to Imogen, who had adored the high life.

'Of course, if you want the right to live in the Pallis world, you've got to share Leonidas and not be possessive.' Imogen tried to act as if she didn't mind watching Leonidas with her replacement, a young film starlet. 'With the choice he's got, you can't expect him to be satisfied with one woman.'

'Just walk away,' Maribel urged ruefully. 'He's a cold, arrogant bastard. Don't do this to yourself.'

'Are you crazy?' Imogen demanded in shrill disbelief. 'I'll settle for whatever I can get from him. Maybe in a few weeks, when he's fed up with the movie star, he'll turn back to me again. I'm somebody when I'm with him and I'm not giving that up!'

And true to her resolve, Imogen's ability to make Leonidas laugh when he was bored ensured that she retained him as a friend. Perhaps only Maribel cringed when she appreciated that Imogen was quite willing to ridicule herself if it amused Leonidas. Then there was a fire at Leonidas' Oxford apartment and Imogen invited him to use her house while she was working abroad.

Maribel's animosity went into override because Leonidas proved to be the house guest from hell. Without a word of apology or prior warning, he took over and moved in his personal staff, including a cook and a valet, not to mention his bodyguards. His security requirements squeezed her out of her comfortable bedroom into an attic room on the second floor. Visitors came and went day and night, while phones rang constantly and scantily clad and often drunken and squabbling women lounged about every room.

After ten days of absolute misery, Maribel lost her temper. Up until that point, she wasn't even sure Leonidas had realised that she was still residing in the house. On the morning of the eleventh day, she confronted him on the landing with a giggling brunette still tucked under one arm.

'May I have a word with you in private?'

A sleek ebony brow elevated, because even at the age of twenty-four Leonidas was a master of the art of pure insolence. 'Why?'

'This is my home as well as Imogen's, and, while I appreciate that in her eyes you can do no wrong, I find you and your lifestyle utterly obnoxious.'

'Get lost,' Leonidas told the brunette with brutal cool.

Studying him in disgust, Maribel shook her head. 'Possibly you are accustomed to living in the equivalent of a brothel where anything goes, but I am not. Tell your women to keep their clothes on. Send them home when they become drunk and offensive. Try to stop them screaming and playing loud music in the middle of the night.'

'You know what you need?' Dark golden eyes hot with a volatile mix of anger and amusement, Leonidas anchored his hands to her hips and hauled her to him, as if she were no more than a doll. 'A proper man in your bed.'

Maribel slapped him so hard her hand went numb, and he reeled back from her in total shock. 'Don't you ever speak to me like that again and don't touch me either!'

'Are you always like this?' Leonidas demanded in raw incredulity.

'No, Leonidas. I'm only like this with you. You bring out the very best in me,' Maribel told him furiously. 'I'm trying to study for my exams…okay? Under this roof, you are not allowed to act like an arrogant, selfish, ill-mannered yob!'

'You really don't like me,' Leonidas breathed in wonderment.

'What's to like?'

'I'll make it up to you—'

'No!' Her interruption was immediate and pungent,

because she was well aware of how he got around the rules with other people. 'You can't buy yourself out of this one. I don't want your money. I just want you to sort this out. I want my bedroom back. I want a peaceful household. There isn't room here for you to have a bunch of live-in staff.'

That evening, she came home to find all her possessions back in her old room and that there was blissful silence. She baked him some Baklava as a thank-you and left it with a note on the table. Two days later, he asked when she was going to pick up his unwashed shirts from the floor. When she explained that her agreement with Imogen did not include such menial duties for guests and that hell would freeze over before she touched his shirts, Leonidas asked how he was supposed to manage without household support.

'Are you really that helpless?' Maribel queried in astonishment.

'I have never been helpless in my life!' Leonidas roared at her.

Of course he *was*—totally helpless in a domestic capacity. But a Pallis male took every challenge to heart and Leonidas felt that he had to prove himself. So he burned out the electric kettle on the hob, ate out for every meal and tried to wash his shirts in the tumble drier. Pity finally stirring, she suggested his staff came back but lived out. An uneasy peace was achieved, for Leonidas could, when he made the effort, charm the birds from the trees. She was surprised to discover that he was actually very clever.

Two days before he moved into his new apartment, he staggered in at dawn hopelessly drunk. Awakened by the noise he made, Maribel got out of bed to lecture him about the evils of alcohol, but was silenced when he told her that it was the anniversary of his sister's death. Shaken, she listened but learned little, as he continually lapsed into Greek before finally commenting that he didn't know why he was confiding in her.

'Because I'm nice and I'm discreet.' Maribel had no illusions that he was confiding in her for any other reason. She knew herself to be plump and plain. But that was still the night when Maribel fell head over heels in love with Leonidas Pallis: when she registered the human being who dwelt beneath the high-gloss sophistication, who could not cope with the emotional turmoil of his bad memories.

The day he moved out, and without any warning of his intention, he kissed her. In the midst of a perfectly harmless dialogue, he brought his mouth down on hers with a hot and hungry demand that shook her rigid. She jerked back from him in amazement and discomfiture. 'No!' she told him with vehemence.

'Seriously?' Leonidas prompted, his disbelief patent.

'Seriously, no.' Her lips still tingling from the forbidden onslaught of his, she backed away from him and laughed to cover her embarrassment. It was her belief that he had kissed her because he had very little idea of how to have a platonic friendship with a woman.

Knowing how Imogen still felt about him, she felt so guilty about that kiss that she confessed to her cousin. Imogen giggled like a drain. 'Someone must've dared Leonidas to do it! I mean, it's not like you've got the looks or the sex appeal to pull him on your own, is it?'

Her earliest memories of Leonidas were bitter-sweet, Maribel acknowledged as her thoughts drifted back to the present. Leonidas had cast a long dark shadow that had somehow always been present during the years that followed. When Maribel had occasionally met him again through Imogen, she had utilised a tart sense of humour as a defence mechanism. While putting together billion-pound business deals, Leonidas had continued to run through an unending succession of gorgeous women and make headlines wherever he went. Imogen, however, had worked less and had become more and more immersed in her destructive party lifestyle. Over a year before her death, Leonidas had stopped taking Imogen's phone calls.

Maribel caught Elias as he ran past her and pulled him onto her lap where he lay, totally convulsed by giggles. Her eyes overbright, she resisted the urge to hug him again and let him wriggle free to return to his play. He was so happy. She did not believe that Leonidas had ever known that kind of happiness or security. Elias depended on her to do what was best for him. She did not believe that any father was better than no father at all; she *refused* to believe that.

Leonidas was conscious of annoyance when he saw Elias Greenaway's birth certificate: he had not been named as the father. 'I want DNA-testing organised immediately.'

The three lawyers seated on the other side of the table tensed in concert. 'Where a couple are unmarried, DNA tests can only be carried out with the mother's consent,' the most senior of the trio imparted. 'As your name isn't on the birth certificate, you don't have parental responsibility either. May I ask if you have a cordial relationship with Miss Greenaway?'

The Greek tycoon's gaze flared gold and veiled. 'It's Dr

Greenaway, and our relationship is not up for discussion. Concentrate on my rights as a parent.'

'Where there is no marriage, the UK legal system favours the mother. If you have the lady's agreement to DNA-testing, to sharing parental responsibility and to granting reasonable access to the child, there won't be a problem,' the lawyer enumerated with quiet clarity. 'Without that agreement, however, there would considerable difficulty. Applying to a court would be your only remedy and, in general, the judge will regard the mother and custodial parent as the best arbiter of the child's interests.'

Always cool under pressure, Leonidas pondered those disconcerting facts, his lean, dark face aloof. Although nobody would have guessed it, he was very surprised by what he was finding out. 'So I need her consent.'

'It would be the most straightforward approach.'

Leonidas recognised what went unsaid but invited no further comment. He knew that there were wheels within wheels. For a man of his wealth, there was always a way of circumventing the rules. When winning was the goal, and it was usually the *only* goal for Leonidas, the concept of fair play had no weight and the innocent often got hurt. That was not, however, the route he wished to follow with Maribel, who had once been sincerely appalled to catch Imogen cheating at a board game. For the moment he was prepared to utilise more conventional means of persuasion…

Maribel lifted her office phone and jerked out of her seat the instant she heard Leonidas' rich, dark-chocolate drawl in her ears. 'What do you want?' she demanded, too rattled to even attempt the polite small talk usually employed at the outset of a conversation.

'I want to talk to you.'

'But we spoke yesterday and I'm at work,' Maribel protested in a near whisper, panic squeezing the life from her vocal cords.

'You're free for an hour before your next tutorial,' Leonidas informed her. 'I'll see you in five minutes.'

Suddenly Maribel wished she were the sort of woman who put on make-up every day, instead of just on high days and holidays. She dug frantically into her bag to find a mirror and brushed her hair, while striving not to notice that her sleepless night was etched on her face and in the heaviness of her eyes. A split-second after that exercise, she was outraged by her instinctive reaction to his phone call. Instead of mustering her wits and concentrating on what was important, she had spent those precious moments fussing over her appearance. A waste of time, she told herself in exasperation, glancing down at her ruffled green shirt, trousers and sensible pumps. Only Cinderella's fairy godmother could have worked a miracle with such unpromisingly practical material.

Leonidas strolled in with the unhurried grace that was so much a part of him. Deceptively indolent dark golden eyes skimmed over her taut expression and he sighed. 'I'm not the enemy, Maribel.'

Maribel lifted her chin, but evaded too close a meeting with his incisive gaze. But that single harried glimpse of his lean strong features still lingered in the back of her mind. The bold, sculpted cheekbones, the imperious blade of a nose and the tough jawline were impressive even before the rest of him was taken into account. She had always got a kick out of looking at Leonidas. Denying that urge to look and enjoy hurt to an almost physical degree.

Desperate to relocate her composure, she sucked in a steadying breath. 'Coming here to see me is indiscreet,' she told him stiffly. 'This is a public building and my place of work. A lot of people would recognise you. You attract too much notice.'

'I cannot help the name I was born with.' His fluid shrug somehow contrived to imply that she was being wildly irrational. 'You must've known that we would have to talk again. Possibly I felt that you would be less likely to threaten me with the police here.'

'Oh, for goodness' sake, you knew I wasn't really going to call the police to get rid of you!' Maribel's patience just snapped at that crack. 'And since when were you afraid of anything? I can see the headlines even as we speak. ATTEMPTED ARREST OF GREEK TYCOON, because you know perfectly well that your bodyguards wouldn't give you up to anybody! Do you really think I would risk inviting that kind of attention?'

'No?' Leonidas filed away the obvious fact that she had a healthy fear of media exposure. Considering the many women who had boasted in print of an intimate association with him, he wondered if he should be offended by her attitude. She had always been so different from the women he was accustomed to that he was never quite sure what she might say or how she might react.

'Of course I wouldn't. I can't believe that you would want that either. In fact I'm sure you've thought seriously about things since yesterday.'

'Obviously.' Leonidas leant back against the edge of her desk and stretched out his long powerful legs, a manoeuvre that had the effect of virtually trapping her by the corner next to the window. The office was no bigger than a large broom cupboard and it contained a second desk because it was a shared facility. He surveyed her with assessing cool. Even tiredness could not dim the crystal clarity of those violet eyes. As for the outfit, it looked drab at first glance, but the snug fit of the shirt and the trousers at breast and hip enhanced the proud curves and intriguing valleys of her fabulously abundant figure. She was woman enough to make many of her sex seem as flat and one-dimensional as cardboard, he conceded, assailed by a highly erotic recollection of Maribel all rosy, warm and luscious at dawn. The instant tightening at his groin almost made him smile, for it was some time since he had reacted to a woman with that much enthusiasm.

Subjected to one sensual flash of his bold, dark golden gaze, Maribel went rigid. She was aghast at the languorous warmth spreading through her and at the swollen feel of her breasts within the confinement of her bra. As her tender nipples tightened she folded her arms in a jerky movement. 'So, if you've thought seriously…'

'I still want answers. At least, be realistic.' His brilliant eyes now screened to a discreet glimmer below lush black lashes, his drawl was as smooth as silk. 'What man would not, in this situation?'

Maribel didn't want to be realistic. She just wanted him to go away again and stop threatening the peace of mind that she had worked so hard to achieve. 'What do I have to do to make you understand?'

'See both sides of the equation. Be the logical woman I know you to be. To ask me to walk away without even knowing whether or not the child is mine is absurd.' The complete calm and quiet of his voice had an almost hypnotic effect on her.

'Yes, but…' Maribel pinned her lips closed on the temptation to speak hasty words '…it's not that simple.'

'Isn't it?' Leonidas countered. 'Clearly *you* believe that Elias is my son. If you didn't believe that, you would have swiftly disabused me of the idea.'

Maribel stiffened, her eyes reflecting her indecision. 'Leonidas…'

'Every child has the right to know who his father is. Until I was seven years old, I believed my father was my mother's first husband. But, after the divorce, it emerged that someone else was the culprit. I know what I'm talking about. Are you planning to lie to Elias?'

'Yes…*no*! Oh, for goodness' sake!' Maribel gasped, raking her chestnut hair off her troubled brow with an anxious hand, as his candour had disarmed her. 'I will do whatever is best for Elias.'

'One day Elias will be an adult, and you will lose him if you lie to him about his parentage.' Leonidas dealt her a cool dark appraisal. 'You hadn't thought of that aspect, had you? Or about the fact that Elias has rights, too.'

Maribel blenched at that unwelcome reminder.

'And what if something happens to you while he is still a child? Who will take care of him then?'

'That's dealt with in my will.'

Any pretence of relaxation abandoned at that admission, Leonidas was as still as a panther about to spring. 'Do I figure in it?'

Tense as a bow string, Maribel slowly shook her head.

The silence folded in as thick and heavy as a fog.

With reluctance, Maribel looked back at him. Leonidas was studying her with a chilling condemnation that cut her to the bone. It was obvious that he had already reached his own conclusions as to her son's parentage. Her heart sank, since she had no way of convincing him otherwise, no magical method of turning back time and ensuring that he did not find out what she had believed he would have been perfectly happy not to know. 'All right,' she said gruffly, her slim shoulders slumping, for she felt as battered as if she had gone ten rounds with a heavyweight boxer. 'You got me pregnant.'

Leonidas was startled by the strong sense of satisfaction that gripped him and relieved that he had not had to exert pressure. As he had anticipated, Maribel had listened to her conscience. So, the boy was his. The boy was a Pallis: the next generation of the family. His ancient trio of great-aunts would be overjoyed at the continuation of the Pallis bloodline, while his more avaricious relatives would be heartbroken at being cut out in the inheritance stakes. Although Leonidas had long since decided that he would neither marry nor reproduce, it had not until that moment occurred to him that he might father a son and heir with so little personal inconvenience.

'I knew that you wouldn't lie to me,' he intoned with approval.

But Maribel felt very much as though she had failed. She knew that decent standards were a weakness in his vicinity. She knew his flaws. Yet she was still ensnared by the stunning gold of his eyes glinting below the dense black fringe of his lashes. He could still take her breath away with one scorching glance.

In a lithe movement Leonidas abandoned his misleadingly casual stance against the desk and straightened his lean, powerful body to his full imposing height. He reached for her taut, clenched fingers, straightening them out with confidence to draw her closer. 'You've done the right thing,' he murmured lazily. 'I respect you for telling me the truth.'

'That's good, because I think that telling you the truth was one of the most pointless things I've ever done.' Her slender fingers trembled in the hold of his as she fought the insidious force of his sensual charisma. Once bitten, for ever shy, she reminded herself frantically. He had almost destroyed her self-esteem more than two years earlier. Imogen and a whole host of other women had somehow managed to do casual with Leonidas, but Maribel had felt as though her heart were being ripped out slowly while she was still alive. And the horror of it had lasted for weeks, months, afterwards.

'How so?' Leonidas could feel the trepidation she was struggling to hide and marvelled at it, for he could think of no reason for her continuing apprehension. His thumb massaging her narrow wrist in a soothing motion, he gazed down at her, his attention lingering on the ripe pink fullness of her mouth. As the rich tide of sexual arousal grasped him he made no attempt to quell it. In fact he was enjoying the astonishing strength of his reaction to her. Seducing Maribel, he was recalling, had been unexpectedly sweet, and it would certainly take care of all the arguments now. 'I'm not angry with you.'

'Not at the moment…no,' Maribel agreed, dry-mouthed, in response to the perceptible change in the atmosphere. Her heart was thumping as fast as a car being revved up on a race track. It was as if time had slowed down, while her every physical sense went on hyper-alert. Her breath catching in her throat, she fought to stay in control.

'We were careless,' Leonidas commented in a husky undertone, wondering if he should lock the door and take full advantage of the moment.

'I wasn't…you were,' Maribel muttered, unable even with her brain in a state of sensual freefall to let him get away with making such an unfair claim.

'I left my wallet in the limo and you wouldn't let me phone for it to be brought in, so I had no contraception—'

'I didn't want your chauffeur and your wretched security team to know what you were doing!' Maribel protested, her cheeks burning at the memory of her embarrassment.

Leonidas gave her a smile of unholy amusement. 'I stayed the night with you. So what?'

'I don't want to talk about it.' Maribel recognised the treacherous intimacy of the discussion. Fighting the wicked draw of his dark animal magnetism, she turned her head away.

He lifted a lean brown hand up to flick a straying strand of amber-coloured hair back from her pale brow. Incredibly aware of his proximity, Maribel quivered. She could feel her whole body leaning towards him. It was as if he had pressed a button and her spine had crumbled. There was a craving in her that overpowered common sense. There was a wild longing for the forbidden and, try as she might, she could not stamp it out.

'You make *this* complicated,' Leonidas muttered thickly, a big hand splaying to the feminine curve of her hip to ease her up against him before she could step out of reach. 'But for me it's simple.'

She knew it was not simple, she knew it was complicated. She even knew that it was a hideous mistake and that she was going to hate herself later. But when he bent his handsome dark head, she still found herself stretching up on tiptoe so that she wouldn't have to wait a split-second longer than necessary to make physical contact. And whatever else Leonidas was, he was an overpoweringly physical male. His lips claimed hers with a red-hot hunger and demand that she felt right down to her toes. His tongue tasted her and she shivered. He pushed against her, banding her closer with strong hands, unashamedly letting her feel the hard thrust of his erection. Answering heat flared low in her belly and she gasped beneath his marauding mouth. Her fingers dug into his broad shoulders. With no recollection of how they had got there, she yanked her hands guiltily off him again. Forcing herself to break free of his arms hurt as much as losing a layer of skin.

Violet-blue eyes blazing with resentment at his nerve, Maribel launched herself clumsily back out of reach. Her shoulders and hips met the filing cabinet behind her and provided merciful support, because her legs felt as sturdy as quaking jelly. 'What the hell are you playing at?' she snapped at him in furious condemnation, angry over her weakness and the hateful inevitability of his having taken advantage of it. 'Is this because I showed you the door at my home yesterday? Did I insult your ego? You have just found out that you're the father of my son! And what do you do? You make a pass at me!'

'Why not?' Having followed his natural inclinations and met with a very encouraging response, Leonidas was in no mood to apologise, particularly not when he was stifling a staggeringly powerful desire to simply haul her back into his arms. 'I think I'm behaving very well. I'm willing to accept responsibility—'

'You've never accepted responsibility for a woman in

your life!' Maribel launched at him with a bitterness she could not conceal.

'I'm willing to accept responsibility for Elias.'

'But you're so busy being a player that you've just shown me all over again why I can't stand the thought of you in my son's life!' Maribel slung at him, the raw force of her emotions ringing from her voice. Her entire body was tingling with almost painful sensitivity and a stark sense of what could only be described as deprivation. Shame over her loss of control threatened to choke her.

'You'll have to learn to stand it and me, because I have no intention of staying out of my child's life.' Hard dark-as-midnight eyes sliced back at her like gleaming rapier blades of warning challenge. 'Elias is a Pallis.'

'No matter what it takes, I swear that I will prevent you from gaining access to him,' Maribel threw back at him with clenched fists.

Leonidas released his breath in a slow, derisive hiss. 'Give me one good reason why you should behave that way.'

'Just look at what being born a Pallis did to you!' Maribel sent him a furious appraisal, because the brazen self-assurance he exuded only reminded her of the dignity she had surrendered in his arms. 'You're irre-sponsible. You have no respect for women. You're a commitment-phobe—'

Derision engulfed by incredulous indignation, Leonidas growled. 'That is outrageous.'

'It's the truth. Right now, Elias would be a novelty to you like a new toy. You only take business seriously. You have no concept of family life or of a child's need for sta-bility. How could you after the way you were raised? I'm not blaming you for your deficiencies,' Maribel told him in a driven undertone. 'But I won't apologise for my need to protect Elias from the damage that you could do.'

Leonidas was pale with fury, his bronzed skin stretched taut over his superb bone structure. 'What do you mean—*deficiencies*?'

'Elias is very precious. What have you got to give him but money? He needs an adult who's willing to put him first, to look after him, but what you cherish most is your freedom. The freedom to do whatever you like when you like would be the first thing you would lose as a father and you wouldn't stick the course for five minutes—'

'Try me!' Leonidas shot back at her in wrathful challenge. 'Who are you to judge me? You have never lived outside your little academic soap-bubble! By what right do you call me irresponsible?'

Although she was drawn and tense, Maribel lifted her head high. 'I've got more right than anyone else I know. You never once called to ask if I was okay after that night we spent together!'

'Why would I have?' Leonidas growled like a bear.

Maribel almost flinched. She refused to allow herself to react in a more personal way and she tucked the hurt of that cruelly casual dismissal away for future reference. 'Because it would have been the responsible thing to do when you knew there was a risk of a pregnancy,' she informed him in a wooden tone.

Leonidas swore in vehement Greek at that retaliation and shot her a censorious glance. 'You walked out on me,' he ground out.

Maribel thought of what had really happened that morning and inwardly squirmed. Walking out would have been the sensible, dignified option, but it was not actually what she had done. He didn't know that, though, and she felt that that fact was none of his business so long after the event. She did not have much pride to conserve over the episode, but what she did have she planned to hang onto.

'It was for you to contact me when you learned that you had conceived,' Leonidas delivered in harsh addition.

'You didn't deserve that amount of consideration,' Maribel told him without hesitation.

Lethal scorn hardened his darkly handsome features. 'I didn't phone—is that what this is all about? So you try to punish me by refusing me contact with my son?'

Maribel looked steadily back at him, her violet blue eyes defiant in the face of that put-down. 'Don't you dare try to twist what I said. Be honest with yourself. Do you really want the hassle of a child in your life?'

Only forty-eight hours earlier, Leonidas would have responded with an unqualified negative to that question. Now a whole new dimension had to be considered. He could not get the image of the smiling little boy in the photograph out of his mind. But his other responses were much more aggressive, because when he looked back at Maribel he could never recall feeling more angry or alienated from her. She had judged him and found him wanting and nobody had ever dared to do that before.

The office door sprang open without warning. 'Why on earth is there a crowd of people hanging around outside?' demanded the older woman with whom Maribel shared the office. 'Oh—sorry. I didn't realise that you had someone with you. Am I interrupting?'

'Not at all,' Leonidas murmured impassively. 'I was about to leave.'

Gripped by a giant wave of frustration, Maribel watched

Leonidas depart. She could not understand why she should feel bereft when he walked away. Her office was no place for emotional discussions. He needed to think about what she had said, as well. Her hand crept up to her lower lip, which was still swollen from the erotic heat of his. It was so typical of Leonidas to try and blur serious issues with sex. He could handle sex. He could handle it beautifully. It was the emotional stuff he couldn't and wouldn't deal with.

Wide-eyed, her colleague hurried back to the doorway. 'Good heavens, was that who I think it is? Was that *actually* Leonidas Pallis?'

A mass of speculative faces peered in at Maribel, as though she were a rare animal on display in a zoo for the first time…

CHAPTER FOUR

MARIBEL could not sleep that night, or indeed during the night that followed.

How long was it since she had fallen in love with Leonidas Pallis? Almost seven years. It sounded like a prison term and had often felt like one, while she'd struggled to feel something—*anything*—for a more suitable man. Her heart might as well have been locked away in a cell, for neither intelligence nor practicality had exercised the smallest influence over what she felt. She had done her utmost to get over him. She knew his every flaw and failing. She did not respect him as a person. Yet helpless sympathy for a male so divorced from his emotions that he did not even recognise grief had led to her lowering her guard after her cousin's funeral. And, to the conception of the son she adored.

Who are you to judge me? She was still pondering that question at dawn on the second day after his latest visit. As she had not expected to see Leonidas again, it had not occurred to her that he would ever find out about Elias. Now that he had, everything had changed and she had been too slow to recognise that truth. Suddenly she was being forced to justify the decisions she had made and she

was no longer confident that she had the right to deny
Elias all contact with his father. Accustomed as she was to
keeping her own counsel, she felt that she was too emo-
tionally involved and that it might be wise to ask for a
second opinion from someone she could trust to be
discreet.

Later that morning, Maribel went over to see Ginny
Bell and finally told the older woman who had fathered her
son.

For the space of an entire minute, the older woman
simply stared back at her with rounded eyes of shock and
disbelief. '*Leonidas Pallis?* The Greek billionaire who's
always plastered all over the celebrity magazines?
Imogen's ex?'

Red as a beetroot, Maribel nodded affirmation.

'My goodness. You do put new meaning into that saying
about being a dark horse!' Ginny exclaimed. 'Leonidas
Pallis is really Elias' father?'

'Yes.'

'I never liked to ask who he was, when you didn't seem
to want to talk about it.' Ginny shook her head in wonderment over what she had just been told. 'I must be frank.
I'm gobsmacked. What prompted you to suddenly tell me
about this now?'

'Leonidas has just found out about Elias and he wants
to see him.' Maribel compressed her lips. 'I've been saying
no.'

Ginny grimaced. 'Surely that's not a good idea, Maribel.
Is it wise to get on the wrong side of a man that powerful?'

'He is very annoyed about my attitude,' Maribel
conceded unhappily.

'If someone told you that you couldn't see your child,

wouldn't you be angry?' the older woman prompted wryly. 'Try to put yourself in his shoes and be fair.'

'That's not easy,' Maribel confided chokily.

'But why run the risk of turning Leonidas into an enemy? Wouldn't that be more dangerous? I've heard some heart-rending stories about children being snatched away by disaffected foreign fathers.'

Ginny could have said nothing more guaranteed to make Maribel's blood run cold in her veins. 'Don't scare me, Ginny.'

'You're playing with some pretty strong emotional issues here. That's why I would try to be reasonable, if I were you.'

'But I think that Leonidas is just curious. I don't see him getting that involved with Elias,' Maribel said tautly. 'Leonidas has never been that fussed about kids.'

The older woman subjected her to a shrewd appraisal. 'You really know Leonidas Pallis very well, don't you?'

Maribel lowered defensive lashes. 'Reasonably well.'

'Then hang onto that bond before you lose it,' Ginny advised ruefully. 'For your son's sake. Some day, Elias will want to know all about his background and he will want to know his father, as well. Making decisions on Elias' behalf is a big responsibility.'

Shamed into reconsidering her stance, but with all her misgivings still very much in place, Maribel went straight back home and phoned Leonidas on his private number. Leonidas answered the call. The instant he heard her voice, he gave his PA a signal that his meeting with his legal team was on hold until he finished the dialogue.

'Maribel,' he murmured smooth and soft.

'All right, you can see Elias. I was being unreasonable. Just let me know when you would like to see him.'

A wave of satisfaction engulfed Leonidas and a rare smile banished the cold set of his lean, strong features. 'I'll send a car to pick you up in an hour. Okay?'

Maribel swallowed. The immediacy of that request disconcerted her and she would've preferred to stage the meeting on familiar ground. On the other hand, Ginny's warnings had unnerved her and she did not want to be awkward. 'It's short notice, but I don't work on Thursdays, so that will be fine.'

'You've pleased me, *glikia mou*,' Leonidas imparted with approval. 'I'll see you later.'

Maribel came off the phone with gritted teeth. She suspected that had she had four legs like Mouse Leonidas might have rewarded her with a pat on the head and a chocolate treat for her obedience. But surely that was better than being at odds with him? She pelted upstairs with Elias to get changed.

A vast limousine complete with an accompanying carload of what appeared to be security guards arrived to pick her up and filled her with dismay. So much for discretion! Fastened into his car seat in the palatial passenger area, Elias took a nap. Garbed in a turquoise skirt and top, Maribel sat with a mirror and did her make-up while attempting not to be impressed by the cream leather upholstery and the built-in array of entertainment equipment. It was some time before she appreciated that possibly she should have asked Leonidas where their meeting was taking place, because the limo did not head into London as she had expected. Her tension increased when the car swept down a long drive and a vast Georgian mansion appeared ahead. Surrounded by rolling parkland that was furnished with stately trees, it was as picture-book perfect as a film set for a historical costume drama.

Resolving not to be intimidated, Maribel balanced Elias on her hip and strolled into a hall the size of a small football pitch. A manservant spread wide a door for her entrance into an exquisitely furnished reception room. She paused to lower Elias to the ground because he was a little squirming, impatient bundle after being cooped up for so long in the car.

Leonidas saw Maribel first and was immediately distracted, for, as she bent over, the neckline of her top gaped to reveal the creamy swell of her full, rounded breasts. Lust took Leonidas instantaneously and infuriated him. Not for the first time, he wondered why it was that a slight provocative glimpse of Maribel's violin curves should have a more powerful effect on him than a full-on striptease. As she straightened, glossy chestnut tresses fanning back to reveal her vivid eyes and pouting raspberry-tinted mouth, he knew he was going to bed her again. But then as the child who had wandered behind her finally came into view and took his attention by storm Leonidas totally forgot what he had been thinking.

'He's so small,' he breathed gruffly.

Her mouth ran dry when she saw Leonidas. On the brink of pointing out that Elias was actually very tall for his age, Maribel also forgot what she was thinking. Leonidas, garbed in well-cut jeans and a coffee-coloured T-shirt teamed with a designer linen jacket, grabbed the entirety of her attention. Black hair brushed back from his brow, and dark, deep-set eyes intent on Elias below level ebony brows, Leonidas looked jaw-droppingly spectacular. Achingly handsome, fashionable and elegant. Suddenly she felt hot and underdressed—and horribly plain.

'Elias!' Maribel called as the little boy tried to climb

over the big square coffee table. He was at an age where he wanted to scale every obstacle in his path.

'Let him enjoy himself,' Leonidas told her with impatience.

The Pallis approach to parenting, Maribel thought, and then scolded herself for being prejudiced. Leonidas crouched down on the other side of the low table. Clambering upright, Elias gave him a huge grin and fell still halfway in his journey towards the elaborate flower arrangement that had attracted his attention. From several feet away, Maribel watched man and boy exchange eye contact. Elias was fearless and full of beans. Leonidas had only to open his arms for Elias to chuckle and run at him, sensing that fun was on offer.

'Man,' Elias pronounced with approval, for there was none in his world.

'Daddy,' Leonidas contradicted without hesitation, resting his broad shoulders back against the sofa behind him to allow Elias to scramble freely over him.

Maribel parted her lips to object and then sealed them shut again. Leonidas lifted Elias up and held him upside down above him. Elias was thrilled by that manoeuvre. Maribel watched in frank fascination while Leonidas, whom she had never seen make an uncool move in his life, engaged in horseplay on the rug with Elias. They ambushed each other round the sofa. Elias got rolled and tossed about and he clearly adored every minute of such robust handling. Feeling superfluous, Maribel sat down on the arm of a chair. She had expected to act as a connecting point, but neither her son nor his father required her encouragement to get to know each other. The discovery that Leonidas could relax to that extent with a young child astonished her.

'He's amazing,' Leonidas pronounced finally. 'What do I do with him now?'

Exhausted by all the excitement, Elias was draped over Leonidas now like a small crumpled blanket.

'He's ready to go to sleep.'

'No problem.' Leonidas vaulted upright. 'I've got a crib waiting for him upstairs.'

'Do you want me to carry him?'

'No. I need to learn how to manage him.'

'You're doing very well for someone who's not used to children.' Maribel accompanied him up the long, elegant stone-and-iron stairway.

'Elias is different. He's mine.'

The bedroom that contained the crib also contained a uniformed nanny, who could just as easily have competed as an entrant in an international beauty contest. A six-foot-tall Nordic blonde with a pearly smile, she took Elias and cooed over him while attending to him with an efficiency that could only impress. Even so, Maribel was dismayed at the speed with which Leonidas had acquired a member of staff to take care of Elias, and said so.

Leonidas shrugged. 'We have to talk. Elias has to sleep and he needs someone to watch over him. Diane has superb references. Loosen the apron strings, *glikia mou*.'

Maribel was mortified. 'Is that what you think?'

'I want to share the responsibility of raising Elias. Stop worrying. You're not on your own any more.'

'But I've managed fine on my own.'

Ignoring that defensive rejoinder, Leonidas rested a lean hand lightly at her spine and walked her to the end of the landing where a giant window overlooked a fabulous view of the parkland. He knew exactly what he was doing and he was determined to win her agreement. If everything went to plan, she and Elias would be flying out to Greece with him the next morning and he would be introducing his son to the family. 'What do you think of Heyward Park?'

'This place?' Her brow furrowed in bemusement. 'It's—it's magnificent.'

Leonidas turned her round to face him. The sudden intimacy in the air took her by surprise and she went pink, insanely conscious of his masculine proximity. His stunning dark golden eyes glittered in his lean, devastatingly handsome face. 'I would like you and Elias to make this your home.'

Shattered by that proposition coming at her right out of the blue, Maribel froze, her brain going into override while she attempted to work out exactly what he meant. But she could think of only one possible interpretation: he was asking her to move in with him! What else could he possibly mean? It was so typical of Leonidas to behave as though the most important issues were quite inconsequential. He understated, rather than overstated, with a dispassionate cool that few could match. 'Leonidas…' she tried to say, but her voice ran out of steam and croaked into silence again.

'Why not?' Leonidas murmured softly, staring steadily down at her while combing her luxuriant hair back from the sides of her face with surprisingly gentle fingers.

Her breath rattled in her constricted throat. He had never set up home with any woman before and she was very much aware of the fact. So were the newspapers and magazines that recycled incessant stories of how ruthlessly he ended his affairs and maintained his unfettered lifestyle.

But then, nobody had taken account of how the advent of one little boy might affect the Pallis outlook. 'You've really taken me by surprise.'

'You're not fighting me any more.' A charismatic smile curved his wide sensual mouth as she gazed up at him with anxious violet-blue eyes. 'I appreciate your generosity.'

Her heart was beating so fast it felt as if it were in her throat. He was only asking her to move in because of Elias. She couldn't accept on those terms; she couldn't possibly. Didn't she have any pride?

'And I also appreciate you *very* much, *glikia mou*,' Leonidas stressed as though he could read her mind. He lowered his arrogant dark head, his breath fanning her cheek. '*Se thelo*…I want you.'

Shaken by that additional declaration, Maribel blinked in confusion. It felt like too much too soon, but Leonidas was very decisive and he always moved fast. It would be stupid, she told herself, to expect a male as forceful an individual as he to behave like everyone else. The faint familiar tang of his cologne flared her nostrils, releasing an intoxicating tide of intimate memory. She felt weak, wicked. A little inner voice warned her to back off and she ignored it, ensnared by the frisson of anticipation coursing through her. He made her feel astonishingly good. He made her feel sexy. He made her feel totally unlike staid, sensible Maribel, and she would not have exchanged the high she was on at that instant for a fortune in gold and diamonds. It was crazy. He had not seen her in over two years and yet he was inviting her to live with him.

'Are you planning to slap me?' Leonidas husked, pressing his expert mouth to a tender pulse point just below her ear and almost making her knees buckle in the process.

Her clutching fingers curled round his lapel to help her

stay upright and tip him towards her. A low-pitched, sexy laugh was dredged from deep in his throat. He toyed with her mouth. She couldn't breathe for excitement, certainly couldn't think. Time hung in suspension while her heart hammered. His tongue slid moistly between her lips in a sensual plunge that stirred a shocking ache between her thighs. That cautionary voice at the back of her mind was jumping up and down and shouting now. *Stop, don't be stupid…it'll end in tears again!* But she could not resist the temptation he offered. Her disobedient fingers dug into his hair and held her to him as she kissed him back with passionate fervour.

Leonidas hauled her up into his arms with more haste than ceremony, as he was determined to take advantage of the moment. One of her shoes fell off and she giggled. She was all passion and high spirits, and he couldn't get enough of her in that mood. He hadn't been able to get enough of her that night he'd slept with her either. She had put a pillow down the centre of the bed and threatened to scream if he dared to cross it again. As he bore her off to the bedroom he was satisfied that he had played a winning hand. He had not been totally confident that she would agree to his scheme. Ninety-nine out of a hundred women would have bitten his arm off in their eagerness to say yes, but Maribel approached every issue with a shopping list of far from flexible expectations. Add in her old-fashioned streak, and when she dug her heels in it could take dynamite to shift her.

A door thudded shut somewhere. Maribel had yet to open her eyes again. He lowered her to a carpet that was soft and silky below the sole of her foot. She kicked off the remaining shoe and snatched in a jagged breath when he released her reddened mouth from the devouring onslaught of his. He was unbuttoning her cotton cardigan. Long brown fingers anchoring in her hair, he tipped her head back. 'Look at me,' he urged thickly. 'I've waited a long time to get you back into my bed.'

Her lashes lifted on dazed violet-blue eyes. Just like that occasion more than two years previously when she had thrown her principles in the rubbish heap, it was all happening too fast for her and doubts were piling up almost as quickly. He nipped at her tender lower lip with his teeth and made her jerk taut with delicious tension. But that tiny pleasure pain reunited her with rational thought and she muttered feverishly, 'Shouldn't we be talking about what you suggested?'

'Later…'

'But…isn't this a very big step for you?' Maribel prompted worriedly.

'*Ne*…yes,' Leonidas confirmed in husky Greek, uneasy with the topic, determined not to go there unless forced. He'd planned to ease her into the arrangement with every atom of guile he possessed and gloss over the imperfections.

'Are you sure about this? That we're what you want?' Maribel whispered with wide, anxious eyes welded to his darkly handsome face.

'Absolutely.'

'But I'm so ordinary,' Maribel muttered, still unable to credit that he was willing to offer her more than she had ever dreamt he might.

'*Filise me*…kiss me,' Leonidas urged, coaxing her lips apart to let his tongue dart with sinuous skill into the sensitive interior of her mouth and wreak havoc with her self-control. Irresistible sensation made Maribel shudder and a whimper of reaction escaped low in her throat.

By the time Leonidas set her back from him, she was trembling. Not quite knowing what to do, she hovered while he unclipped her bra. Last time she had had two glasses of wine, a lot of turbulent emotion and a sense of recklessness to get her to the brink of intimacy. But guilt and an unplanned pregnancy had given her an instinctive fear of her wanton inner woman and when the swollen bounty of her breasts spilled free of the lace cups his guttural groan of masculine approval only fired self-conscious crimson colour into her cheeks.

'You are magnificent, *mali mou*.'

Maribel still felt incredibly unsure of herself. But then he touched her with strong male hands and helpless physical response enfolded her, stopping her thoughts in their tracks. He moulded the firm creamy mounds and chafed the pouting pink buds that crowned them. His every caress sent tiny little tremors through her while a velvet knot of heat and anticipation uncoiled in her belly. He toyed with her tender nipples and lowered his mouth there to tease the lush, straining tips. Delicious tension gripped her until she was breathing in shallow little gasps, her entire body boneless with simmering, tingling pleasure.

'This is not how I imagined today would turn out,' she confessed unsteadily, a kind of wonder finally daring to blossom inside her and become joy.

Gorgeous golden eyes hot as flames on her oval face, Leonidas tipped her back on the bed. 'Set your imagination free. Today and every day can be what you want it to be now, *mali mou*.'

'Wish-fulfilment,' Maribel muttered, a slim hand curving to a long, powerful male thigh.

'My wish at this precise moment is to be very dominant,

and for you to lie there and allow me to pleasure you,' Leonidas husked in a roughened undertone.

He eased up her skirt in a slow, erotic manoeuvre and nudged her nerveless legs apart. She could feel herself melting like butter beneath a blow torch. Long before he could reach the sweet, damp warmth between her thighs, her excitement was at screaming pitch. Her languorous purplish-blue gaze clung to his bold dark features. 'This once,' she traded unevenly, 'I shall just lie here and think of living with you.'

Leonidas saw disaster hovering on the horizon and almost cursed out loud in his seething frustration. Avoiding the discussion of detail was one thing; lying an impossibility. He rolled over and pinned her in place beneath a muscular thigh. 'We won't be living together,' he murmured. 'This will be your home with Elias and I'll stay only when I'm visiting.'

Visiting? Maribel felt herself freeze in self-protection from the giant rolling wave of pain threatening her composure. Her sense of rejection was acute, but as nothing next to the awful sense of humiliation she experienced. She felt as though she had been slapped in the face with her own stupidity, for he had no desire whatsoever to live with her. He simply wanted to house his son in a luxury dwelling where he could conveniently visit him and occasionally enjoy a little recreational sex with his son's mother. By no stretch of the imagination was he offering her a normal relationship or indeed any form of commitment towards a shared future. Shutting her eyes tight, she tried to pull free of him.

'No…no, you're *not* bolting on me again!' Leonidas growled, catching both her frantic hands in his and pinning them above her head in one of his to hold her in place. 'Calm down.'

'I'm calm,' Maribel declared.

'I'm sorry if I misled you.'

'Let go of me,' she framed tightly between compressed lips.

'Sometimes I could stay the whole weekend with you. Maybe we could even share the occasional vacation,' Leonidas proffered, holding her wildly squirming body captive with the considerable weight of his own. 'It would be good. It would be a very efficient arrangement.'

The last drop of hope inside her died when he voiced that passion-killing word, 'efficient'. 'If you don't let me up, I'll scream.'

Leonidas would much have preferred a scream to the frozen tension of her face and the flatness of her voice. He coiled back from her with extreme reluctance.

Wrapping a screening arm over her bared breasts, tears burning like acid behind her lowered lashes, Maribel slid off the bed, snatched up her discarded clothing and headed straight for the adjoining bathroom. 'I'd appreciate it if you would wait for me downstairs.'

'*Theos mou*…why are you being so bloody unreasonable about this?' Leonidas demanded, vaulting off the bed in one powerful movement. 'Anyone would think I'd insulted you!'

Maribel almost lost her head with him at that point. Had there been anything suitable within reach she would have snatched it up and thrown it at him with vicious intent. Mercifully there wasn't, and she shut the door behind her and simply stared blankly into space. When was she going to learn to keep her distance? Only an idiot would have credited that Leonidas Pallis was offering her a serious live-in relationship. Her eyes burned as she fought back the tears with all her strength. She had almost ended up in bed with him again. Concentrate on the positive, her intelligence told her, not on your mistakes. She could not afford to let go of her emotions. She had to face him again, still had to deal with how two such disparate people—one of whom was a domineering, selfish, spoiled billionaire—could possibly share the upbringing of one little boy.

The instant Maribel entered the drawing room, Leonidas swung round, but before he could say anything she spoke. 'Let's just concentrate on Elias—'

'*Theos mou*, Maribel—'

'That's the only business we have to discuss. We should avoid anything of a more personal nature.'

Leonidas dealt her a fulminating appraisal. 'Elias is not business.'

'Elias is the only reason I am still in this house and speaking to you,' Maribel confided jerkily.

'Very well.' His strong jawline clenched. 'I would like DNA-testing to be done, not because I doubt that Elias is my son, but because there should be no room for any person to doubt that he is a Pallis.'

'All right,' Maribel conceded.

'I would also like your support in having his birth certificate changed to carry my name.'

'If you feel it's necessary.' Although Maribel was feeling totally devastated after what had happened between them, she was doing her utmost to conceal the fact. But it was a challenge to behave normally, when even looking at his lean, strong face actually hurt her. 'Anything else?'

'I'm attending a family wedding tomorrow in Athens,' Leonidas informed her. 'I would like you and Elias to accompany me as my guests. I plan to introduce him to my relatives.'

Maribel stiffened into the defensive mode she had been striving to hold at bay. 'We can't come. Apart from anything else, I'm working tomorrow—'

'I'll take Elias and the nanny, then,' Leonidas traded without hesitation. And she noticed, could really not help noticing, how quickly he was able to dispense with the concept of having her as a companion.

'He's too young to leave me and I won't agree to you taking him out of the country without me. I'm sorry, but that's the way it is for the present,' Maribel told him, her hands lacing restively together when she saw the grim tension tighten his fantastic bone structure. 'I will try to be reasonable in other ways, though. But I would ask you to think again about telling people that you have a son.'

'You have a problem with that, as well?' Leonidas shot back at her, his anger at that request palpable.

'I would prefer it to stay a secret for as long as possible. The press attention and public notice that it would generate could make my life with Elias very difficult.'

'That is precisely why I suggested that you live in one of my properties where your security needs can be met without fuss.'

'But we won't have security needs if you let your connection to Elias remain a private one. I would appreciate it if my life could go on the same way it always has—'

'That's no longer possible.'

'You're not being fair to me,' she protested.

'Less than half an hour ago—for the *right* offer—you were willing to surrender all autonomy over your life, your job and your child.' Leonidas voiced that reminder with derisive emphasis.

Maribel went white at the biting cruelty of that statement. The misunderstanding had mortified her, and only courage stiffened her backbone. 'More fool me,' she muttered with scorn. 'To believe, for even five minutes, that you would make that much of a commitment to either Elias or me! You don't even recognise when I'm trying to be generous—'

'*Generous?*' Leonidas threw up lean brown hands in forceful disagreement. 'When you even object to me taking him to my home in Greece? How is that generous?'

'You're lucky I'm still here after that sleazy proposition you put to me!'

'It was not sleazy. Naturally, I would prefer my son to live in a manner appropriate to his status. I want to take care of both of you.'

'No, you don't. You want the ability to play father any time you like at the cost of *my* freedom—oh, yes, and occasional sex. Was that to keep me happy? Stop me from looking around for long enough to give Elias a stepfather?' she demanded in disgust. 'Or was it just a power-play or a power lay? You *would* sleep with me because you *could*?'

Those twin offensive cracks about stepfathers and power lays sent raw fury roaring through his lean, powerful frame. 'I've offered you more than I have ever offered a woman,' Leonidas intoned with disdain, outraged by her attack.

'But not any kind of a promise that might curtail your freedom. And without that it was a rotten, lousy offer. Elias needs caring and commitment. I'm sorry, but there's no short cut and no quick fix to supplying those. Do you really think that a casual affair with your son's mother would give him a stable, happy home? It wouldn't last five minutes, and when it broke down Elias would suffer. You can't buy access to him through me.'

The coldness of displeasure had hardened the Greek tycoon's bold bronzed features. His dark, deep-set eyes were like black ice. 'I asked you once before not to make this a battle, for whatever it takes I will win.'

As no doubt intended, the threat Maribel perceived in that assurance slid like an ice cube down her rigid spine and settled in her belly, sparking nausea. Fear of losing her son sliced through her, and with it came fierce anger that he should dare to subject her to that level of anxiety. 'And you wonder why I wouldn't even consider letting you take Elias to Greece? Forget the DNA-testing and any change to his birth certificate!' she told him vehemently. 'You have just ensured that I will obstruct any claim you try to make on Elias.'

A white-hot blaze of wrath engulfed Leonidas. He strode forward, the chill in his gaze a formidable warning. 'I won't let you keep me apart from my son. It is madness for you to oppose me in this way. I expected much more from you.'

Stubborn as a mule in the face of intimidation, Maribel stood her ground and surveyed him with furious blue eyes. 'I have to admit that I'm getting more or less what I expected from you. You haven't changed.'

'But you still want me, *glikia mou*,' Leonidas countered silkily. 'I should have appreciated that your sexual compliance would have a major price tag attached. How ambitious are you?'

His sheer insolence made her palms tingle with incipient violence. 'Meaning?'

'Why not put your cards on the table? Were you hoping that I might eventually ask you to marry me?'

A brittle laugh of disagreement was wrenched from Maribel's tight throat. 'No! I don't live in fantasy land. But I must confess that only a wedding ring would now persuade me that I can trust you with my son.'

Leonidas dealt her a sizzling look of derision.

'That was a fact, not a suggestion,' Maribel told him tautly. 'Right now I'm very conscious that you could use your influence and financial power to put pressure on me, but I won't be intimidated. I'll still let you see Elias, but that's all. I don't trust you. I won't give you the chance to take him away from me. I will not let my child out of my sight for five minutes around you, or your employees!'

Leonidas was inflamed by those pledges. He was a responsible adult and Elias was his son. Her attitude incensed him.

A knock on the door interrupted the dialogue. It was Diane, the nanny, with Elias. Sleepy and fretful after waking up in a different room, the little boy held out his arms to his mother. 'Mouse…Mouse,' he muttered tearfully, seeking the security of the familiar pet.

'You'll see Mouse later,' Maribel soothed, folding him close.

'Is Mouse a toy?' Leonidas demanded.

'The dog. '

'You should have brought him.'

Maribel said nothing but almost heaved a sigh. Leonidas was a Pallis and from birth he had been accustomed to instant wish-fulfilment. People went to great lengths to please him and satisfy his every desire. That was not the way she wanted Elias to grow up.

'I'll show him the stables,' Leonidas drawled icily. 'He'll enjoy seeing the horses.'

Maribel nodded without looking near him. 'I'd like to go home at six. It's a long drive back.'

Elias wriggled and squirmed until she lowered him to the rug. He pelted across it to Leonidas and stretched up his arms to be lifted. Hoisted high, he chuckled with pleasure. Even though Maribel knew it was nonsensical, she felt rejected and hurt.

CHAPTER FIVE

LEONIDAS looked down at the old farmhouse as his helicopter flew over the roof to land in the paddock at its side. It was a filthy, wet, windy day and he was in an equally filthy mood. A month had passed since his war of words with Maribel at Heyward Park.

Since then, Leonidas had seen Elias on average twice a week, but it had taken a massive amount of planning to achieve that frequency and he still only managed to see his son for a couple of hours each time at most. Travelling back and forth to Maribel's isolated country home entailed considerable inconvenience and discomfort. Leonidas had not, however, uttered a single complaint. A saint could not have faulted his unfailing courtesy and consideration.

Yet Maribel avoided him during his visits, which made it impossible for him to achieve a better understanding with her. At the same time, his legal team's delicate efforts to negotiate more practical access arrangements had run into a wall of refusal. One month on, nothing had changed: he could see his son only at the farmhouse and could not take him out. He brooded on his conviction that Maribel was hoping he would eventually get fed up and go away.

The racket of the helicopter flying overhead drove

Maribel naked and dripping from the shower. Wrapping a towel round herself, she raced downstairs and found the telephone answer-machine flashing that a message had been received. She didn't waste time trying to listen to it. Evidently Leonidas had made a last-minute decision to visit and, of course, it wouldn't have occurred to him that she might have other plans. Elias, who had already worked out that the sound of a helicopter always signified the arrival of his father, was bouncing up and down as if Santa Claus were about to come down the chimney. She pelted back upstairs and dragged a comb ruthlessly through her wet hair while simultaneously pulling out clothes. She'd only got her panties on before the doorbell went. In feverish haste, she climbed into her jeans. The bell went twice more while she struggled to pull them up to fasten them at her waist. She ran out to the landing and bawled downstairs, 'Give me a minute!'

Elias was whinging with the same appalling impatience on his side of the front door. She yanked on a T-shirt and raced down barefoot.

'Thank you,' Leonidas drawled in a long-suffering tone.

Rattled by his inopportune arrival, Maribel made the very great mistake of allowing herself to look directly at him for the first time in a month of vigilant self-restraint. And that one imprudent glance at him knocked her sideways: he looked amazing. Raindrops glistened on his black hair and classic olive-toned features. His brilliant dark eyes glinted below heavy lashes, his strong masculine jawline and beautifully shaped mouth accentuated by the faint bluish-black shadow where he shaved. Her tummy not only flipped, but performed a series of rapid somersaults.

'I wasn't expecting you—I was in the shower,' she

mumbled, fighting a belated defence action with all her might. Stop it, stop right now, her inner voice of sense was warning her. Don't look at him and don't respond to him, he's pure poison and heartache in a very dangerous package.

'Didn't my staff contact you?'

'I only came home ten minutes ago. I haven't had time to check my messages yet.'

'Your mobile?'

'Forgot to charge it.' As Maribel turned away to close the door his attention was hooked by the distinctly erotic ripple of her voluptuous breasts, which were moulded to perfection by a T-shirt that clung so lovingly to her damp skin that he could see the swell of her pouting nipples. His lean, well-built body reacted with rampant male enthusiasm. He could not shake the deep inner conviction that if he just got her back into bed everything would be perfect.

Maribel watched Elias clawing his way up Leonidas's trouser-legs like a mini-mountaineer. Elias already adored his father. Helped up to chest level, the little boy wrapped two plump arms round Leonidas and covered his face with enthusiastic kisses. He was a very affectionate child, but Leonidas was unused to such physical demonstrations of warmth and liking. The first time Elias had kissed him, Leonidas had frozen in shock. But now Leonidas was trying to reciprocate with occasional awkward hugs. It hurt Maribel to watch, as she knew that Leonidas didn't know how to show or return affection because he had not received it as a child. If anyone was capable of teaching Leonidas how to love another human being, it was her son. That was good, that was healthy. Unfortunately, the more signs of attachment Maribel saw developing between father and son, the more fearful she became of what Leonidas might do in the future.

Maribel would not let herself look again at Leonidas because she was fiercely determined to detach herself from feeling any personal response to him. She had a date, she reminded herself furiously; she was going out on a date in just over an hour. Sloan was an attractive, eligible guy, a research assistant, only a couple of years older than she was. Until Leonidas had arrived, she had been looking forward to the prospect of adult company.

Mouse the wolfhound peered out from below the table and whined in excitement. On his belly, he crawled into view with his long tail banging noisily on the floorboards in a show of ingratiating fervour. Once all of his long grey shaggy body had emerged, Leonidas tossed him a dog treat in reward. Mouse guzzled it down and fixed adoring doggie eyes on his new idol. Maribel didn't think that Leonidas had ever had anything to do with dogs before, either. But once he had registered how important Mouse was to his son, Leonidas had mounted an edible charm offensive to lessen the animal's terror of strangers. And, in common with most challenges that Leonidas set out to meet, he had achieved his goal with brilliance. Bribery, Maribel reflected grimly, worked even in the canine world.

'I have to talk to you,' Leonidas murmured with quiet insistence. 'I can't stay long. I have a flight to catch in a couple of hours.'

'That's good because I'm going out.' Maribel managed a stony smile in his general direction, while remaining wildly and insanely conscious of his every tiny movement. He was so graceful he literally drew the eye to him, and that was even before she noticed the faint husk of his breathing and the dark chocolate tones of his deep sexy voice. 'What do you think we need to talk about?'

Leonidas took up a commanding stance by the fireplace. 'You have to trust me not to try and take Elias away from you.'

'How can I?' Dismay at the directness of that opening salvo made Maribel fall still. 'You've never shared anything in your life; you've never had to. You are number one in all your relationships. It's the Pallis way.'

'Naturally I have to share my son with his mother. I am not an idiot,' Leonidas traded dryly.

'But I'm not doing what you want me to do. Sooner or later, you might persuade yourself that you're entitled to *all*, rather than half, of your son and you could decide to write me out of the picture. You will assure yourself that I have brought that misfortune on myself by my unreasonable behaviour.'

'Where do you get the idea that you know how I think? Or what I might do?' Leonidas demanded with freezing disdain.

Yet, if truth were told, Leonidas was disconcerted by her ability to tap into the deep vein of ruthlessness that powered his aggressive instincts. But he was angered by her flat refusal to accept that Elias stood outside the usual parameters his father observed. Why had she yet to notice that he was making a laudable and heroic effort to put Elias' needs, rather than his own, first?

'Seven years of watching you operate from close up and from a distance?' Maribel shot back at him tightly, torn by conflicting impulses, for when she heard that sincere note in his voice, and watched him unbend with Elias and laugh and smile, she found it hard to say no to him and even harder to police his every move. But two weeks earlier she had taken the precaution of seeking legal advice from a very expensive London solicitor. He had pointed out that Leonidas had almost unlimited power and influence and had advised her to watch over Elias at all times; the law would be of little help if her son were to be taken to a country without a reciprocal agreement to respect UK law.

Leonidas settled level dark, deep-set eyes on her. 'I will give you my word of honour that I will not attempt to remove him from your care.'

Framed by dense black lashes, his eyes had stunning impact, a strong and charismatic key to the level of his sleek, darkly handsome attraction. No matter how hard she tried, her heart was hammering behind her ribcage and her gaze stayed welded to him even as her cheeks burned with colour. 'I can't trust you. I'm sorry. I can't. He means everything in the world to me.'

'He needs you. He's still a baby. I understand that,' Leonidas intoned, strolling lithely closer.

Maribel grew so tense her knees trembled beneath her. 'But he won't always be a baby and I can't keep on changing the rules.'

'If you insist on making rules I'll break them or go round them, *mali mou*,' Leonidas imparted huskily, dark eyes shimmering slices of golden enticement below his lashes. 'I'm made that way.'

'But as I found out that time that you stayed with me in Imogen's house when we were students,' Maribel muttered in a breathless rush, like a deer with a lion stalking around it in an ever-decreasing circle, 'you can follow rules beautifully if it suits you to do so.'

'Maybe I was scared you would slap me again.' The

sexual provocation of his slow-burning smile was an erotic work of art.

Her mouth ran dry. A pulse seemed to be beating low in her tummy. Excitement was building, tensing her every muscle. And then she remembered Sloan and she went into instant retreat, ashamed and angry over her weakness in Leonidas' vicinity. 'I have to get ready. I have a date.'

Lean, hard-boned face taut, Leonidas frowned. 'You have a *date*?'

Still backing, Maribel nodded in vigorous confirmation. 'So if you don't mind I'll go back upstairs and leave you with Elias.'

The atmosphere was heavy, ultra-quiet.

'Okay?' Maribel pressed uneasily.

Pale beneath his bronzed skin, Leonidas fixed his attention on a distant point beyond the window. She had taken him by surprise. But what took him even more by surprise was the tide of anger flooding him. 'Who is this guy?'

'I don't think that's any of your business,' Maribel almost whispered.

Leonidas thought of several very unreasonable responses to that statement. He relived the insulting way in which she had backed away from him. Had that ever happened to him with a woman before? His lean, strong features darkened and set in hard, angular lines. He had been tempted to yank her back to him. He reminded himself that it was not his way to be possessive with a woman. But then Maribel was different, he reasoned just as quickly. Maribel was in a class of her own. Surely it was understandable that he found the very idea of his son's mother becoming intimate with another man deeply objectionable? Elias was tugging at his raincoat now to get his attention. Leonidas had to make an effort to show an interest in the toy train being extended for his admiration. Thinking of how her boyfriend might get to spend time with his son gave Leonidas another cast-iron reason for loathing the whole concept of such a relationship.

His silence in response to a defiant answer shook Maribel rigid, but she didn't quarrel with the reprieve. She hurried away to get dressed. Keen to avoid Leonidas, she even painted her nails to use up more time. Only when she heard Ginny's car pulling up outside did she hasten down-stairs to answer the door.

As Maribel reappeared Leonidas glanced up and, in ten seconds flat, minutely catalogued the amount of effort Maribel had made to prepare for her outing. Much more effort than she had ever made for his benefit, he decided, lethal antagonism building on the anger still seething below his unemotional surface. In fact, she had gone to town on her appearance: perfume, chestnut hair straight-ened into a smooth fall round her pale pink luscious mouth, a pastel girlie top, peach-tinted nails, shapely legs on view in a swirly skirt, sexy high heels.

'This is Ginny Bell, my friend and neighbour who will be looking after Elias while I'm out. Ginny, this is Leonidas Pallis.'

Only when Maribel spoke did Leonidas take note of the woman who had followed her into the room. He rose silently up to his full height. The dark-haired older woman by Maribel's side was staring at him as if she couldn't quite believe her eyes. Agitated as a jumping bean, Maribel watched Leonidas switch on his effortless social charm and wondered anxiously why he had gone so quiet with her earlier. If he was displeased, quietness was in no way typical

of Leonidas. Ginny was bowled over by him, couldn't hide
the fact and chattered. Leonidas soon established that
Maribel was attending a wedding party and was expected
home late, so Ginny was staying the night. His mood was
not improved by that information, or by the enthusiasm
with which Maribel rushed outside before her date could
even get his car door open and put in an appearance.

When Leonidas left five minutes after Maribel's speedy
departure, rage was sitting like a hard black stone at the heart
of him and consuming more of his thoughts with every
second that passed. As he headed back to the helicopter Vasos
called him on his mobile. His bodyguards, who had watched
the farmhouse while he was inside, converged on him.

'I've had a tip-off,' his security chief told him. 'A tabloid
newspaper has a lead on Dr Greenaway and the child. You
have the connections to kill the story at this stage.'

Shrewd intelligence glittered in Leonidas' hard dark
eyes. He pictured the farmhouse under siege by the paparazzi. The press would go crazy: A SECRET HEIR TO THE
PALLIS BILLIONS? There would be no place to hide from the
storm of publicity and speculation. Maribel would need his
help to handle that attention. She would also need somewhere to stay, for there was no way that she could be ade-
quately protected in her current location. Before she knew
where she was, she would be putting down roots at
Heyward Park, alongside Elias and Mouse and the moth-
eaten poultry collection. Satisfaction at that prospect lifted
the chilling shadow from his lean, strong face.

'I don't want the story killed.'

'You *don't*?' Vasos was startled, as he was well-ac-
quainted with his employer's loathing for the endless press
coverage of his private life.

'We'll use the same source to feed back certain facts. I'll sue if there's any hint of sleaze. Dr Greenaway and my son will also require surveillance and protection from this moment on.' Having referred for the first time to Elias as his son, Leonidas slid his phone back in his pocket. He knew he was being a bastard. But Maribel would never find out. What she didn't know wouldn't hurt her. All that mattered was the bottom line.

In the early hours of the following morning, Maribel slid her shoes off her aching feet, locked up and crept upstairs as quietly as she could.

Tired and disheartened, she acknowledged that she had faked her every smile with Sloan. From the moment Leonidas had arrived and stolen her attention, her chances of having a good time with Sloan had gone downhill fast. She hated herself for the fact. But the relentless pull of Leonidas' attraction had broken through her barriers again.

As she got into bed she reflected that Imogen had never got over Leonidas either and losing the entrée to his exclusive world had devastated her. Only near the end of her cousin's life had Maribel learned that it was Leonidas who had persuaded Imogen to enter rehab; not only had he paid for it, but he'd also settled all her debts at the same time. Only after Imogen had twice abandoned her treatment programme had Leonidas stopped returning her calls.

His grim reserve on the day when Imogen had been buried had warned Maribel that he was finding the occasion a trial. That was the day when she had finally realised that she was surprisingly good at reading Leonidas, who struck other people as utterly unfathomable. At the funeral, she had also noticed his aversion to sycophantic strangers and the women trying to chat him up. He had spoken to her several times while assiduously ignoring everyone else.

Her aunt had asked her to go on and clear out Imogen's house. By then, Maribel had had her own apartment, although she had often stayed with her cousin to look after her. In fact, during that last year, all Maribel's free time had gone into watching over her troubled relative. After the funeral, Maribel had felt bereft, and when she'd reached the house she'd found it in a mess: Imogen's sisters had already sacked her wardrobe and rummaged through every cupboard, taking what they wanted, leaving Maribel to tidy up and dispose of what was left. Maribel had wandered round the silent house and, when she'd come on some old photos, had cried unashamedly while allowing herself to remember the good times.

Leonidas' arrival had been a total bolt from the blue.

'I knew you would be here. You're the only one who genuinely cared about Imo.' Sombre and magnificent in his black suit and overcoat, Leonidas skimmed a knuckle gently across Maribel's tear-streaked cheek and frowned down at her in reproof. 'You feel like ice.'

'I left my coat at my aunt's and the house is cold.'

With a ceremonial flourish, Leonidas removed his coat and draped it round her shoulders. He signalled one of the men stationed by the limo and addressed him in Greek. While she hovered in bewilderment, the gas fire in the front room was lit.

'You should have a brandy.'

'The drinks cabinet was cleaned out a long time ago.'

Leonidas issued another instruction. Within ten minutes

she was sipping a brandy and warming up inside and out. She was further disconcerted when he began talking about the first time Imogen introduced him to her. He was the only person who seemed to understand the depth of her attachment to her cousin.

'Why are you here?' Maribel finally asked.

'I don't know.'

And Maribel saw that he didn't recognise or understand the grief and sense of regret that had prompted him to come to Imogen's house and talk about the past. His incomprehension of his own emotions somehow pierced her to the heart that day.

'It was an impulse,' he finally added. 'You were very upset at the funeral.'

Afterwards, she told herself that the brandy she'd drunk went straight to her head. Of course, there'd also been the exhilaration of Leonidas' full attention and the delight of almost drowning in the sensuality of his kiss. How they'd got upstairs to the guest room that had once been hers, she could not recall. Nothing had seemed to matter but the moment. For a few brief hours she had discovered a happiness more intense than any she had ever known. But the next morning she'd felt terrifyingly scared and oversensitive. His mocking request for breakfast, as though they had shared only the most casual encounter, had hurt like salt in a wound. But had she learnt even then?

No, she had raced out to buy food, as there had been nothing to eat in the entire house. But it had been a foggy morning and, before she'd even reached the supermarket, someone had rammed their car into the back of hers and she'd been injured. It had been hours before she'd recovered consciousness in a hospital bed.

* * *

Two days later, Maribel was wakened by the doorbell.

Assuming it was a special postal delivery, she sighed and got up. The phone started ringing as she opened the door. It was a shock when a bunch of people she had never seen before began running across the lawn towards her shouting and waving cameras. She slammed the door shut again so fast she bashed a microphone being extended towards her.

Her mind blank with shock, she snatched up the phone.

'It's Ginny. My sister phoned me. There's a front-page story on you and Elias in *The Globe*!'

'Oh, no!' Maribel stared in horror at a man peering in through the living-room window at her. She flew over to close the curtains. 'There's a crowd of people in the garden. They must be reporters.'

'I'm coming over. You can't possibly bring Elias to me this morning.'

Someone was knocking on the back door. Every window seemed to have a face at it. She ran around frantically closing curtains and blinds. The phone rang again. It was a well-known female journalist asking if Maribel wanted to sell her story for a substantial cash payment.

'I mean, from what I can see,' the woman commented cheekily, 'Leonidas Pallis isn't exactly keeping you in the luxury you deserve.'

That call was followed by another of a similar ilk, and then she unplugged the phone. Elias had climbed out of his cot and seated himself at the top of the stairs to await a storm of maternal protest over his athletic achievement. Big dark brown eyes alight with curiosity, he watched his mother race about instead in a panic. A hand rapped on the narrow window beside the front door. Maribel ignored it, but nerves were making her feel nauseous. The hubbub outside her quiet and peaceful home horrified her. Mouse would be having a panic attack in his kennel with all those strangers around.

As she pulled on her clothes at speed she peered out through the side of her bedroom curtains and fell still in surprise. Three large thickset men in smart suits were practising crowd control and forcing the photographers to back away from the house itself into the lane. She recognised one of the men as a member of Leonidas' security team. How had they got here so fast? Not that she wasn't grateful for the support, she conceded ruefully.

Her mobile buzzed while she was trying to keep Elias in one place long enough to get a pair of trousers on him. It was Leonidas.

'I understand the press are harassing you, *glikia mou*,' he murmured with audible sympathy.

'It's a nightmare! But your men are out there making them stay back from the doors and windows, which is quite an improvement,' Maribel confided in a rush, feeling in charity with him for the first time in weeks. 'I'm amazed that your bodyguards were able to get here so quickly.'

'The paparazzi are very persistent. You won't find it easy to shake them off. It's a big story.'

'Fortunately, Ginny will be here soon to look after Elias, and now I have the protection of your heavy mob. I'm going to work in half an hour.'

At the other end of the line, Leonidas almost groaned out loud at her innocence. Like a little train on a single track, Maribel would stick stubbornly to her routine, no matter what happened. 'They'll follow you there. Some of my staff will take you. I don't want you trying to drive with those guys tailing you.'

'No, thanks for the offer. But bodyguards would stick out like a sore thumb,' Maribel told him gently.

'I think you may find it very difficult to remain at your home. It might be a good idea to consider a move to Heyward Park.'

Maribel stiffened. 'I don't run at the first sign of trouble, Leonidas.'

'You can't keep Elias locked up out of sight for ever.'

At that salient point, Maribel's face shadowed and she came off the phone in an even more troubled mood.

Ginny arrived while she was giving Elias his breakfast and settled a newspaper on the table. 'There's the article. I decided to buy a copy before I came over. Let me finish feeding Elias. Where did the heavies come from?'

'Heavies? Oh, Leonidas' security men.'

'I should've guessed. They're very professional. They checked me out before they would let me approach the door. It's bedlam out there, though. I don't envy you trying to go to work with a posse behind you.'

BILLIONAIRE BABY BOY! the headline screamed. Maribel was too busy reading the lead story to respond to her friend. An old photo of her taken some years earlier at one of Imogen's parties made her eyes widen. She wondered how on earth it had been obtained and the more she read, the more confused she became. Instead of the shock-horror lies, half-truths and errors she had expected, all her background details were correct, right down to the little-known fact that her late father had been an award-winning scientist who'd chosen academia over financial gain. She was described as a long-standing and trusted confidante of Leonidas Pallis and she rolled her eyes to the ceiling, wondering who had dreamt up that whopper. When had Leonidas ever confided in anyone?

'The article is all right,' Ginny commented. 'It's surprisingly tame and kind. You sound like a cross between Einstein and Leonidas' best friend.'

'It's a disaster,' Maribel muttered wearily. 'I'll never be taken seriously again in the ancient history department.'

Her friend gave her a wry look. 'Don't underestimate the effect of having a very close connection to one of the wealthiest men in the world. Some of your colleagues will be deeply envious and others will suck up to you. Anyway, it's time you went to work. Elias will be safe here with me and Leonidas' men.'

Maribel found it a real challenge to leave her home and drive away with cameras popping and flashing and questions being shouted at her. When she arrived at the department there were more journalists waiting. A crowd began forming around her before she even got upstairs to her office. Even people she knew were stopping and staring and she hated every minute of the attention. Her small tutorial group was uneasy with the number of interruptions that occurred. She couldn't concentrate either. When she emerged from her office in the late afternoon, she had to almost force her passage back out to her car, which was surrounded by photographers urging her to give them a chance to take a decent picture of her. By the time she got away, her hands were trembling on the wheel and her brow was damp with perspiration. Her heart sank when she turned up the lane to her house and saw that there were even more paparazzi encamped than there had been at the start of the day. She was very grateful when the Pallis security team cleared her path to the house.

Ginny was still sitting behind closed curtains in a dim interior. Mouse was now indoors but in a pitiable state, shaking all over and refusing to come out from below the table. Elias had curled up with the dog. Maribel picked him up and cuddled him.

'I'm rather puzzled about something,' Ginny remarked. 'I made coffee for the bodyguards. What do you think I found out?'

'Tell me.'

'One of them let drop that they were detailed to work here the day before yesterday.'

Maribel gave her friend her full attention. 'But that's not possible.'

'Someone must've known in advance that that story was in the pipeline. Leonidas' men were here ready and waiting for the balloon to go up.'

Maribel became very still. It was as if the circuits in her brain were connecting to show her an unexpected pattern. Mental alarm bells began jangling. One too many inconsistencies in recent events forced her to reconsider all of them. Leonidas had been remarkably mild about the paparazzi invasion, and astonishingly tactful and unassuming when he had merely suggested that she should consider moving into his Georgian mansion. Mildness, tact and humility were not typical Pallis traits. In addition, the personal information in the article had been staggeringly accurate and the tone unusually benevolent. That she should suspect Leonidas of prior knowledge and even of having had a hand in destroying her anonymity struck Maribel as appalling. But the suspicion also roused her furious indignation and a strong need to know the truth beyond all doubt.

'Ginny…could you bear to stay here alone with Elias until later this evening?' Maribel asked tautly. 'I need to see Leonidas.'

CHAPTER SIX

MARIBEL was in the private lift being wafted up to Leonidas' office in the Pallis building when her mobile rang. It was Hermione Stratton, and her aunt was in a virulent fury.

'Is it true that Leonidas Pallis is the father of your son?' Hermione demanded in a furious voice of disbelief.

Maribel winced; she had always feared that that revelation might annoy the older woman. 'I'm afraid so.'

'You sly, scheming little witch!' her aunt condemned shrilly. 'He couldn't possibly have wanted you. You couldn't hold a candle to Imogen in looks or personality!'

That verbal onslaught from her closest relative gutted Maribel. 'I know,' she responded gruffly. 'I'm sorry that you've been upset by all this.'

'Don't make me sick! Why would you be sorry? That little boy must be worth a fortune to you! You've been a very, very clever young woman.'

'I think I've been rather stupid,' her niece contradicted in a pained undertone. 'I didn't plan this. This is not how I wanted my life to turn out.'

'Don't you dare get in touch with anyone in this family ever again!' the older woman warned her in a vitriolic rant. 'As far as we're concerned, from this moment on, you're dead.'

After those harsh words, Maribel was pale as snow. She had hoped that time would soften her aunt's attitude to her son and could now see no prospect of that. The lift opened onto a private vestibule. A male PA ushered her into a huge office and informed her that Leonidas would join her when his early-evening meeting had finished. The tall windows displayed the most amazing views of the City of London, lights twinkling against the backdrop of a ruddy sunset. The furniture was contemporary and stylish. First and foremost, however, it was an efficient, custom-designed workspace. Leonidas never mixed business with pleasure. He would probably be less than pleased at her uninvited descent on his business empire.

'Maribel…' Lean, mean and magnificent in a tailored grey pinstripe suit that was enlivened by a red tie, Leonidas wore a rare expression of concern on his darkly handsome features. In a disconcerting move, he crossed the room and reached for both her hands. 'You should have told me that you wanted to see me. I would have sent a helicopter to pick you up. How are you?'

He was a class act, she acknowledged abstractedly, never stuck for the right word for the occasion. In collision with his brilliant dark heavily lashed eyes, she felt positively dizzy. As always, he looked amazing and he made her feel detached from reality, breathless, on the edge of thrills too wicked and wonderful to even think about without blushing. Yet, she had only to think of her son and there was murder in her heart when she gazed back at Leonidas.

'You're being nice because you believe you've won.

You think I've come running all this way in search of your support, don't you?' Maribel bit out shakily, powered by rage and wounded pride.

'Isn't that what I'm here for?' Leonidas surveyed her with resolute cool and satisfaction, for he could think of nothing more appropriate than that she should demand and expect his assistance. Her independence in a crisis infuriated him. 'You've had a very distressing day.'

Maribel snatched her hands free of his in a gesture of rejection. 'Isn't that how you planned it?'

His ebony brows drew together. 'Naturally not.'

'But you were the instigator of that story in *The Globe*,' Maribel fired at him without even pausing to draw breath. 'You were behind it. No, don't you *dare* lie to me!'

Displaying a disturbing amount of confidence in the face of her livid attack, Leonidas lounged back against his designer desk with lithe grace. 'I have never lied to you.'

Maribel spun away from him, literally so angry she couldn't speak. But even turned away from him she could feel the power of him. Nobody could be around Leonidas without becoming aware of the extent of that strength and power. 'The article in the paper was too precise. All the facts were right and there were no scandalous revelations.'

'There is no scandal in your life,' Leonidas pointed out gently. 'Apart from me.'

Angry, incredulous suspicion had brought Maribel to London to confront Leonidas. At the very core of her, though, there had still been room for healthy doubt and an acceptance that sometimes a chain of coincidences could give a misleading impression. But she had accused him and he had not yet voiced a word of denial in his own defence.

Not one single word. The meaning of his silence on that score was finally sinking in on her.

'You did mastermind it—you *were* behind that story about us,' she whispered unevenly. 'It's hard for me to accept that even you could be that selfish and destructive.'

Leonidas was determined not to rise to the bait. He hoped he was not unreasonable: Maribel was entitled to feel aggrieved and he was prepared to let her get that out of her system. While curious as to how she had worked it all out so fast, he was by no means surprised by her swift grasp of the truth. Shimmering dark-as-ebony eyes screened, he scrutinised her, admiring the natural pink of her cheeks and the generous curve of her mouth. Long before he got as far as the ravishing swell of her abundant breasts, his groin was tightening. He was disconcerted by the speed of his response.

'The paparazzi were already onto us,' he pointed out.

'There is no us!' Maribel shot back at him angrily.

'Are you saying that because you're seeing someone else? And don't tell me that's nothing to do with me,' Leonidas urged. 'It is relevant to this situation.'

'I'm not currently involved with anyone else,' Maribel admitted grudgingly.

'Whether you like it or not, we have a connection through our son,' Leonidas asserted in the same outrageously quiet tone. 'How long did you think I could keep on flying down to see Elias without attracting attention? He could not be kept a secret indefinitely, *glikia mou.*'

'I disagree—'

'But—with respect—you don't know what you're talking about. You don't live in my world. It's a goldfish bowl. Even with all my staff and security, my movements are watched and noted in the gossip columns. Sometimes it is wiser to handle the press and shape what is published. The alternative is often a hatchet job, and I felt that when it came to you and my son a sensitive PR spin on the facts was preferable.' Leonidas viewed her with immense calm. 'I stand by that decision.'

Her violet eyes blazed with resentment. She could not credit the extent of his nerve. 'Stop wrapping it up and trying to pretend that you did it to protect us! You weren't planning to tell me the truth and you don't seem to understand or care how much damage you've done!'

At that condemnation, his chiselled jawline clenched. 'I appreciate your annoyance.'

'Like you appreciate me as "a confidante"?' Maribel slammed back at him with scornful force.

The faintest hint of dark blood demarcated the superb slant of his cheekbones. 'You're angry, but my intentions were good. I'm not ashamed of Elias. He's my son. I'm proud of him. I refuse to hide him.'

A shaken and humourless laugh was dredged from Maribel's lush pink lips. The most colossal sense of bitterness was overtaking her. 'And what about our lives? That aspect didn't matter to you, did it? But my privacy has been destroyed and you had no right to do that. I will for ever be associated with a tacky one-night stand and you—'

All relaxation jettisoned, Leonidas strode forward. '*Theos mou*—that night was neither of those things.'

Maribel wasn't listening. 'Wasn't it enough that I let you see Elias? Does everything have to be your way?'

'I want both of you in my life on an open and honest basis,' Leonidas informed her boldly.

'And if you can't get what you want by asking, you'll fight dirty?' Maribel was starting to tremble with rage. 'All you've done is prove how right I was to distrust you. I'm finished with you, absolutely, totally finished. I gave you a chance and you blew it—'

'You, not I, made this a fight. I won't walk away from either of you.'

'You've been walking away from women all your life and, right at this moment, the son that you pretend to value so much is hiding under the table with the dog!' Her blue eyes were glistening with wrathful tears of condemnation, her anger all-consuming. 'Elias doesn't understand why I'm unhappy, why the curtains can't be opened, why it's dark, why it's so noisy outside, or why he can't go out to play the way he usually does. He's scared and he's upset. You are his father and you did that to him today.'

Leonidas had paled below the healthy bronze of his complexion.

'And why did you do it?' Maribel breathed fiercely. 'Because you are an arrogant bastard, who can't see past winning. Well, today, you lost, Leonidas. You scored a spectacular own goal. I can't trust you. I'm afraid now. You're a threat to me and to my son. You'd have to marry me to see Elias again.'

His ebony brows snapped together. 'What the hell are you talking about?'

'Because that's the only way I could ever feel safe letting you have access to him again! I don't have the resources or the connections to stand up to you. Only a wife could fight you on the same level. As we both know, that's not going to happen, so please leave us alone. With a bit of luck the paparazzi will then get bored and go away. I have no wish to live in the public eye.'

Leonidas was stunned by her attitude. 'You can't bar me from your lives.'

'Why not? I've seen what you can do with your money and your influence. It's my duty to protect my son and I can't compete with you—'

'Elias does not need to be protected from me!' Leonidas closed his hands over her narrow wrists to prevent her backing away from him.

'Doesn't he? What sort of an influence will you be?' Maribel almost sobbed, for rage and sorrow had melded into a combustible mix inside her. 'You own dozens of houses, but you've never lived in a proper home. Even as a child you didn't have rules, you just did as you liked. You had a miniature Ferrari and your own race track at ten years old. You can't give Elias or teach him what you never knew yourself.'

'If you move in Heyward Park and stop being so stubborn and difficult, *mali mou*,' Leonidas breathed in a raw undertone, 'I might learn. That is, if I have anything to learn, and I am not convinced that I do.'

Scorching dark golden eyes blazed down into hers and sentenced her to stillness. There was a sob locked in her throat and a maelstrom of emotion fighting for an exit inside her slim, taut figure. She would never be happy in a casual living arrangement of that nature. He was an addiction she needed to cure, not surrender to. While she adored Elias, she believed that she would have been happier had she never met his father. 'I want my life back. A clean break.'

'No.' Long brown fingers meshed into the fall of her

chestnut hair to angle her head back. He brought his arrogant dark head down and grazed the tender skin of her throat with his lips and the edge of his teeth. Her every skin cell jangled into vibrant, energetic life and an achingly sharp pang of pleasure-pain tightened low in her tummy.

For a split-second Maribel wanted Leonidas so much it hurt. In a devastating burst of intimate images she recalled the passionate weight of his lean, strong body over hers that night in her cousin's house. A passion that had cost her so much she was still paying for it. Just as quickly she remembered her aunt's verbal attack. When was enough enough? Stinging tears at the back of her mortified eyes, she mustered her self-discipline and she pulled free of him. Her oval face was pale and tight with self-control.

'No,' Maribel told him in flat refusal. 'You're bad news for me.'

No woman had ever told Leonidas that he was bad news before.

'I've said all I've got to say.' Maribel walked back to the door, all churned up inside and frozen on the outside. 'Stay away from us. I don't owe you anything. Only a few weeks ago you didn't know Elias existed and you were perfectly happy and content. I wish you had never come to visit me. You lifted the lid on Pandora's box.'

Leonidas stared with brooding intensity at the space Maribel had so recently occupied. She had walked out on him—*again*. Savage frustration roared through his big powerful frame. So, he had got it wrong. Badly wrong. It was exceedingly rare, but he had made a mistake and he was prepared to acknowledge the fact. Why was she always judging him? Even worse, finding serious fault? Walking away, refusing to compromise or even negotiate?

What did it take to please Maribel? If it was a wedding ring, she was destined to disappointment, he reflected harshly, dark eyes hard as iron. What kind of blackmail was that? His chilling anger was tempered, however, by the picture he could not get out of his head—his son taking refuge beneath the table with that pathetic dog. It felt very much like an own goal and that galled him. But what honed his anger to a gleaming razor edge was the knowledge that without Maribel's permission he could not even see Elias.

A week crept past on leaden feet for Maribel.

She was surrounded and ambushed by paparazzi at home and wherever she went. At her request, the police restricted the press presence to gathering at the foot of the lane, but she was still afraid to take Elias into the garden lest a stray photographer pop up from behind the hedge or the fence. She was also tormented by the fear that she had been unfair to Leonidas who, after all, was what he was because he had been horribly neglected as a small child.

In Maribel's opinion, his late mother, Elora Pallis, had had no more notion of how to be a parent than a shop-window dummy. An only child, the volatile heiress to the Pallis fortune of her generation, Elora had racked up four marriages and countless affairs before she'd died of a heart attack in her mid thirties. Non-stop scandal and drug and alcohol addiction had ensured that Elora was a poor mother to the daughter born while she was still a teenager and the son born three years later. Leonidas had only found out who his true father was after the man had died. He had received little in the way of love, attention or stability. When he was fourteen, he had gone to court to demand legal separation from his capricious mother and had moved in with his grandfather. Within three years, however, his mother, his older sister and his grandfather had passed away leaving him alone. And alone was what Leonidas had been ever since, Maribel conceded heavily. At least, until he had met Elias.

Eight days after their London meeting, Leonidas strode into Maribel's office in the ancient history department when she was labouring over a timetable.

'Leonidas?' she queried in stark disconcertion, rising hurriedly upright behind her cluttered desk. Her heart was pounding uncomfortably fast because her once rock-solid nerves had taken a real battering since the paparazzi had begun chasing her around.

Although the lean sculpted face was austere and his dark, deep-set eyes hard as granite, his breathtaking attraction still made the breath catch in her throat. 'If marriage is the only way, I'll make you my wife.'

Shock took Maribel by storm as this was not a development she had foreseen. 'But I wasn't serious…I was only making my point.'

Leonidas looked grimmer than ever and unimpressed by her claim. 'Elias is a powerful incentive. I'm suggesting a business arrangement, of course.'

'Of course,' she echoed, not really sure she knew what she was saying, or indeed what she was feeling, beyond a sense of unreality. 'How could a marriage be a business arrangement?'

'What else could it be? I want access to my son. I want him to have my name. I want to watch him grow up. You won't share him without a wedding ring. I recognise a deal when I get offered one, *glikia mou*.'

'But that's not what I meant. I simply want what is best for Elias.'

Leonidas elevated an imperious brow. 'Yes or no? I will not ask twice.'

Maribel thought very fast. If she married him, she would be giving him legal binding rights over Elias, but she would be around to curb any parenting excesses and watch over her son. If the relationship went wrong she would at least be able to afford the services of a good lawyer. Those were the practical considerations, but what about the personal ones? A business arrangement could only mean that he was talking about a platonic relationship.

Those acquainted with the fabled Pallis cool and control would have been astonished to learn that, at that precise moment, Leonidas was hanging onto his temper by a very slender thread. He had just done what he had always said he would never do: he had proposed marriage. A gold-digger would have accepted before he even finished speaking. A woman who cared about him would have displayed some generous and warm response, he reasoned fiercely. But what was Maribel doing? Mulling the offer over with a serious frown on her face!

Marrying a guy who didn't love her, and who would probably despise her for marrying him on such terms, would not be a ticket to happiness, Maribel ruminated ruefully. It would be a stony road full of disappointments and hurts. So, what was new? On the other hand, if she was destined never to love anyone else, she might as well be with him as be without him. Surely any marriage would be what *she* made of it? Looking to Leonidas to make a constructive matrimonial input would be naïve and foolish.

It would be like unlocking a lion's cage and expecting the predator to come out and behave like a domestic pussycat. Leonidas had had no positive marital role models. Not only did he not have a clue, but she would have to contend with the unhappy truth that he had no intention of changing.

'Yes,' Maribel said gravely. 'I'll marry you.'

'With reservations?' he derided softly.

'Plenty,' she admitted without hesitation. 'I'm a realist and you're unpredictable.'

Leonidas studied her with brooding dark eyes that now glittered like ice crystals. 'I want the wedding to take place in three weeks.'

Maribel blinked. 'Only three weeks from now? For goodness' sake, Leonidas—'

'It'll get it over with. My staff will make the arrangements.'

Maribel worried at the soft underside of her lower lip, her eloquent eyes veiled to hide her discomfiture. *It'll get it over with.* She now knew all she needed to know about Leonidas' view of marriage and it did nothing for her self-esteem.

'I'm off to New York tomorrow,' Leonidas imparted. 'It'll be at least two weeks before I'm back in the UK. I have other stuff to take care of. If you and Elias come to London today, I'll be able to spend some time with him before I leave.'

'Yes...all right.' Her agreement was swift for she had never felt comfortable about keeping father and son apart.

'You'll be spending the night with me.'

Her soft lips parted as though she would have said something, but then finding her mind blank of inspiration, she closed her mouth again. For an instant, she thought he might just mean that she was to stay beneath the same roof, but there was an intimate light in his brilliant eyes that told her otherwise. A dulled flush of awareness illuminated her creamy skin. 'Just like that?'

'I'm not waiting for the wedding night,' Leonidas told her with disdain.

But Maribel was rather confused, for she had reached the conclusion that the marriage he was suggesting was one of convenience alone. 'A business arrangement that includes…er…*sharing a bed*?'

'Think of it as a deal sweetener, *hara mou*.' Leonidas advised, smooth as the most expensive silk. 'Once you've shared my bed, I know you won't back out on me.'

Maribel veiled her expressive gaze, lest he see the growing bewilderment etched there. A marriage that was a business arrangement—of the most intimate sort? And why would she back out? She was not in the habit of last-minute changes of heart. For possibly the first time it dawned on her that Leonidas did not trust her either, and she was surprised by how hurtful she found that discovery.

Long brown fingers tipped up her chin. 'Have we a deal?'

Hot enough to feel as though she were burning up, Maribel gave him a self-conscious nod of confirmation. He lifted her hand and she watched in surprise as he slid a magnificent ruby and diamond ring onto her engagement finger. The jewels shone with dazzling brilliance. 'If I have to do this, I'll respect the conventions,' he breathed curtly. 'This, like the wedding, is part of the surface show.'

Any thrill she might have received from the ring was swiftly squashed by that assurance. It did not even feel like a personal gift; it felt more like a prop she was being allowed to wear for the sake of appearances. 'I'm amazed that you care about the conventions.'

'But you do, and when I say I'll do something, I do it right and I deliver on my side of the bargain.' His keen, curiously forbidding gaze whipped over her taut and troubled face. 'I hope you're equally thorough in the wife stakes.'

Blue eyes sparkling violet at that challenge, Maribel suppressed her misgivings and murmured, 'No doubt you'll soon tell me if I'm not.'

Without warning an appreciative grin slashed his perfectly shaped masculine mouth, instantly putting to flight his icy aura of unapproachability. He bent his handsome dark head and, for a split-second, she actually thought he might be about to kiss her. But he frowned instead and checked his watch. 'A helicopter will pick you up at home at two.'

Maribel nodded slowly. She was so stunned by the idea of marrying him that she was in a daze. 'This doesn't feel real yet.'

Leonidas dealt her a caustic appraisal. 'It'll feel real soon enough. A word of warning—I'll make a lousy husband.'

With that attitude, Maribel believed that this was very probable and she wondered if she was mad to have agreed. After all, he was only willing to make that commitment for his son's sake. The door flipped on his exit, only to be caught before it could close again. Her tutorial group trooped in. She spared a glance down at the enormous ring. It was really exquisite. But essentially meaningless, she reminded herself doggedly, determined not to succumb to any silly flights of fancy.

CHAPTER SEVEN

THE penthouse apartment that Leonidas occupied in central London seemed gigantic to Maribel. A manservant led her across the vast limestone floor of the striking foyer and ushered her into an even bigger reception area.

In the doorway, she set Elias down on his feet. He looked adorable in pale blue cord trousers and a little cotton shirt. Before her eyes could adjust to the bright daylight that flooded in through the long run of windows that comprised the farthest wall, Elias loosed a squeal of excitement and yanked his fingers free of his mother's grasp.

'Daddy!' he yelled, sturdy little legs carrying him across the room in seconds.

A vision of casual elegance in a loose beige linen shirt and chinos, Leonidas scooped the little boy up and closed both arms round him. He was startled by the tide of emotion coursing through him. Elias gave him a big soppy kiss and then struggled to get down again, eager to investigate the mysteries of a strange room.

'He missed you. He asked for you a couple of times,' Maribel admitted guiltily.

Leonidas studied her with keen attention. She had that

refined quality of quintessential Englishness that he had always admired and never quite managed to define to his own satisfaction. Her lustrous chestnut hair was a shining frame for her delicately modelled features and, while her outfit was plain, her simple blue dress threw her violet eyes into amazing prominence. She had a subtle unusual beauty as authentic as her lush sex appeal and he could not understand why it had taken him so long to acknowledge the fact. After all, she had always had the most disturbing knack of immediately attracting his attention even in a crowd.

'Why are you staring at me?' Mirabel muttered uneasily, wondering if she should have used more make-up and put on fancier clothes

'I like the dress, *hara mou*. Of course, I'll like you even better out of it,' Leonidas confided, his dark, rich drawl taking on a husky edge. 'By the way, how has the boyfriend dealt with the relentless pursuit of the paparazzi?'

Her cheeks flaming at that unashamed reminder of the night ahead, Maribel veiled her gaze at that question and jerked a slim shoulder in silent dismissal. Sloan hadn't phoned again and she didn't blame him for the fact. The amount of press interest she was currently drawing, not to mention the exposure of her association with Leonidas, would have scared off the keenest of blokes. The last time she had seen Sloan, he had been gaping in horror at the spectacle of her trying to outrun the photographers to make a fast getaway in her car.

Leonidas got the message that the competition had been decimated and he returned his attention to Elias with a sat-isfied gleam in his dark gaze that would have chilled a block of ice. In the best of humour, he introduced Elias to the toy ride-on car he had bought for him. Elias was ecstatic and got straight into making noisy vroom-vroom sounds and punching the horn and an array of tempting buttons with vigour. While Leonidas was trying not to flinch at the racket, he found himself wondering if Maribel had slept with the boyfriend. He wondered in some bewilderment why he was wondering, but it was far from being the end of that disquieting thought-train, because he was soon wondering how many men there had been since she'd walked out on him two years and two months earlier. Although he continued to devote his attention to his son, all Leonidas' relaxation and satisfaction had drained away.

Lounging back on a gilded sofa with her shoes kicked off for comfort a few hours later, Maribel watched Leonidas roll out a convoy of boats for his son's bath-time entertainment. For a Greek tycoon, whose fortune was based on a vast shipping empire, she supposed an entire fleet was a natural choice, and, certainly, Elias was impressed. Quite deliberately, Maribel was staying in the background. She had tried to leave father and son alone for a while, but Elias, for all his apparent confidence, still needed to check that his mother was present every so often. On the one occasion that Maribel had dared to rove out of sight, her son had shocked Leonidas by screaming the place down. Yet Leonidas was marvellous with Elias and comfortable playing with him. In fact, Leonidas was demonstrating a level of patience and calm with his son that Maribel had never dreamt he possessed.

She was in a guest bathroom large enough to run to several pieces of furniture in addition to the usual fixtures. A stray glimpse of herself in a mirror on the nearest wall made her tense. Her face was pink because she was warm, her hair tumbled, the illusion of straight, smooth locks destroyed by the damp atmosphere that was reviving her natural waves. She stared in dismay, thinking of how ordinary she looked against the grand backdrop, how incongruous a match she was for Leonidas with his jaw-dropping good looks. The idea that she had been fighting day and night since Hermione Stratton's upsetting phone call crept in: Imogen would have looked so much more at home.

For a dangerous moment, Maribel pictured her late cousin, garbed in a designer frock and reclining along the same sofa. With her curtain of silvery blonde hair draped across one shoulder and a mocking smile on her beautiful face, Imogen would have maintained a flow of entertaining chatter. Amusing men had come naturally to her cousin. It was only thanks to Imogen that Maribel had ever met Leonidas Pallis, and if Leonidas had not decided he needed company after Imogen's funeral, Elias would never have been conceived. A sharp pang of discomfiture and unhappiness attacked Maribel as she made herself confront those humiliating truths.

Springing upright, Leonidas hit the call button on the wall and opened the door to Diane, the nanny, whom he had summoned to take over. While Elias was distracted by the new arrival, Leonidas bent down to close a hand over Maribel's and tug her off the sofa and out into the corridor.

Dragged without warning from her troubled thoughts and her comfortable seat, she spluttered, 'I left my shoes in there—'

'You won't need shoes where you're going,' Leonidas told her bluntly.

'But Elias—'

'He's falling asleep sitting upright! But if he kicks up

a fuss, Diane will call us, *hara mou.*' As Maribel hovered indecisively Leonidas scooped her up into his arms to forestall further protest.

As a manservant stepped back against the wall out of his employer's path, Maribel felt totally annihilated by embarrassment. 'Leonidas, it's barely eight o'clock in the evening!' she hissed in a frantic whisper.

'I like to take my time.' Coming to a halt in a spectacular bedroom, Leonidas slid her slowly down the length of his long, lean body.

Just as quickly, brought into lingering physical contact with his strong muscled frame, Maribel was intensely conscious of his potent masculinity. As her breasts rubbed against his broad chest their sensitive peaks tingled. Her stomach grazed the hard, flat slab of his abdomen and his big hands welded to the generous curve of her hips to bring her even closer. Registering the rampant evidence of his desire sent a wanton thrill of anticipation winging through her. Her cheeks flushed with fiery colour, she hid her face against his shirt. It was still damp from Elias' antics in the bath, but Leonidas had the body heat of a furnace and the linen was drying fast. The hard-muscled warmth of his lithe, powerful form and the intrinsically familiar scent of his skin filled her with a sensual awareness that left her legs as weak as matchsticks.

Long fingers speared through her tumbled amber coloured hair to tug her head back. 'I like your hair longer—the way you used to have it. Grow it for me,' Leonidas instructed softly.

'You can't tell me how to wear my hair,' Maribel told him tautly.

'Why not?' His level dark golden eyes didn't leave hers

for a single second. For emphasis he scored her cheekbone with a reproachful forefinger. 'Don't you want to please me?'

'Do you want to please me?' she dared.

'*Ne*—yes, but I don't need any pointers, *mali mou.*'

'But you think that I do?'

'You can't learn if I don't teach you,' Leonidas countered soft and low, his tone eminently reasonable.

'This doesn't sound like much of an equal partnership.'

'I'm a Greek. I have a traditional outlook. So you grow your hair again,' Leonidas repeated, impervious to hints. 'It will be charming.'

His powerful gaze held her as effectively as a chain round her ankle.

'Is this, like, Lesson One in the How-to-be-a-good-little-Pallis-wife course?' Maribel dared unsteadily.

'If you want to think of it that way.' Cupping her *derrière*, Leonidas lifted her against him. 'But there haven't been any good little wives in my immediate family for a long time.'

She was holding her breath even before he bent his handsome dark head and claimed a devouring kiss. Sensation ravished her senses. She found the taste of him utterly seductive. There was a delirious intimacy to the way he made love to her mouth. Tiny shivers darted up and down her spine. Her hands clenched as she held back out of pride from just grabbing him. With the tip of his tongue he explored and delved in the tender interior until she was pushing back against his lean, hard body in helpless, gasping response.

Leonidas pulled free, scanning her with hot golden eyes before he spun her round. He was struggling to rein back his desire, as it had naturally occurred to him that her walkout more than two years earlier might have been her understandable reaction to a less than successful introduction to sex. Although she had acted as though everything was amazing, he was uneasily aware of her predilection for politeness. That sliver of doubt that he had buried since their love-making was beginning to haunt him again because, if that was the problem, he wanted to know. He ran down the zip on her dress and skimmed it very slowly down over her arms while he used his expert mouth to trace a pattern across the tender skin at the nape of her neck.

'Oh-h-h…' Trembling, Maribel closed her eyes and let the tiny little shivers of delicious response ripple through her and gather momentum. At that instant, she could not find an ounce of decent resistance or restraint. Her knees were wobbling. She was melting from inside out.

'I'll make it spectacular, *hara mou*,' Leonidas told her.

A surge of love laced with reluctant amusement overwhelmed Maribel: Leonidas would never knowingly undersell himself.

'Maybe it wasn't quite spectacular the last time,' Leonidas breathed without warning.

Her dreamy eyes shot wide in surprise and she whispered uncertainly, 'I never said that.'

Leonidas was tense. He noticed that she was not contradicting him and he wondered why the hell he had embarked on such a dialogue. It was not his style. 'You were a virgin. It was unlikely to be perfect.'

Maribel flipped round in the circle of his arms and before she could think better of the impulse said, 'I thought it was.'

Dense black lashes lifted on his tawny eyes. 'The first time?'

Even that first times she realised helplessly, but she

didn't think he needed or deserved that ego-boosting information.

Leonidas saw no reason to enquire further. *Perfect?* That rare and very disturbing moment of sexual self-doubt evaporated like a bad dream. His tension banished, he crushed the rosy pouting curve of her lips under his and sent her dress shimmying down to her ankles in a superbly choreographed manoeuvre that came very naturally to a male of his extensive experience. Disposing of the band of lace covering her lush, creamy breasts, he backed her down onto the big bed before she had even registered it was gone.

'You're seriously good at this stuff,' Maribel told him helplessly, feeling shamefully exposed and wonderfully decadent at one and the same time.

Shedding his shirt, Leonidas sent her a wolfish smile that was pure provocation. She watched him stroll back to her and her breath tripped in her throat. He was beautifully built, with wide, bronzed shoulders, a hard, muscular chest and long, powerful legs. He paused to peel off his trousers. The aggressive bulge of his arousal was clearly delineated by his boxers and burning pink blossomed in her cheeks. She felt she should look away and she couldn't. Tantalising heat tingled between her thighs and she pressed them together guiltily. That night, at Imogen's house, she had not even seen him undress, for things had got out of hand incredibly fast after he'd kissed her. They had made love in the dark, on top of the bed, still half dressed, too wild with passion and impatience to take their time. Never in her life had she imagined she could be like that with a man, feel like that, or even behave like that. It was only now that she was even allowing herself to remember how it had been.

Leonidas studied Maribel with raw masculine appreciation. She was all creamy opulence and soft ripe curves. He noticed the abstracted look in her gaze. 'What are you thinking about?'

'That night…er…at Imogen's house.' His unexpected question drew a more honest answer from her than she would have given, had she had forewarning.

'You ripped my shirt off me, *hara mou*…' His smouldering appraisal flamed reflective gold.

'Did I?' Maribel mumbled in a stifled tone, since she had hoped that he had long since forgotten that kind of detail.

'It was mind-blowing…it was the hottest sex I ever had.' After the unchallenged passage of that all-forgiving word, 'perfect', Leonidas was finally willing to concede that fact.

Cheeks fiery, Maribel studied her bare feet.

Leonidas came down beside her and pulled her close with a possessive hand. He lowered his tousled dark head to the inviting swell of her glorious breasts. He teased a straining rosy crest with his lips. He pressed her back and flicked his tongue skilfully over its twin to coax an ever stronger reaction from her. Her fingers sank into the silky black depths of his hair and she gasped, her throat extending. There was a throbbing pulse at the slick centre of her body, beating out the longing that she had suppressed since they were last together. Now her ability to hold back her hunger was being destroyed piece by piece.

'I want my tigress back, *mali mou*,' Leonidas husked, nipping at the base of her ear with his even white teeth, guiding her hand down to the hot velvety length of his erection.

Her slim fingers flexed round his hard male heat. A

sense of vulnerability and the dread that she might be in danger of giving away too much warred with her desire. She truly loved touching him, and adored the intimacy and the thrill of sending him out of control. But, in the aftermath of the one night they had shared, she had also fallen victim to a whole host of humiliating fears. Had she been too bold? Too clumsy in her inexperience? Too keen?

Leonidas groaned out loud. Hot pleasure was shot through with the sudden darkling suspicion that she might have been practising. Anger stirred and sharply disconcerted him, forcing him to shut out the thought. Even so, he slid out of reach of her ministrations.

'What's wrong?' Concerned eyes as purplish a blue as violets questioned him.

'Nothing.' But Leonidas was uneasy with the disturbingly irrational thoughts and responses assailing him. Highly intelligent and pragmatic by nature, he rejoiced in the benefits of cold logic. He had never felt possessive of a woman in his life.

There was hurt and confusion in Maribel's gaze now. With a stifled curse in Greek, Leonidas drove her reddened lips apart in a ravenous kiss that sent her anxiety flying like skittles out of sight and out of memory. Each plunge of his tongue only stoked her yearning higher. A little clenching frisson low in her pelvis made her press closer to him, seeking relief from the ache thrumming at the heart of her desire. She was quivering with that almost agonising awareness long before he removed her last garment to discover the damp, delicate folds beneath.

'*Se thelo*…I want you, *hara mou*,' he breathed in a driven undertone.

'I want you too,' she whispered feverishly.

A whimper of sound halfway between protest and delight was wrenched from her when he stroked the most sensitive place of all. Very soon, she was lost in the dark, pulsing pleasure that he unleashed. Perspiration dampening her creamy skin, she writhed in moaning response to the flood of erotic sensation of which he was so much the master. She was caught up in the irresistible surge of exhilaration. Her blood was hammering through her veins, her heart pounding. Bewitched by his touch, in thrall to his strong sensuality, she was all liquid warmth and seething frustration. Her desire reached a bitter-sweet edge of torment for she could not bear to wait another moment for fulfilment.

In that same instant, Leonidas slid between her thighs. Supplication in her passion-glazed eyes, she was shaking and shivering, pitched to an almost painful pinnacle of need. He entered her at the peak of that longing. Bold and powerful, he forged an entrance into her hot, wet sheath. A surge of ravishing sensation engulfed her for the feel of him within her melting flesh was exquisite. He kissed her and she responded with all the wild passion consuming her. He delved and teased her mouth with his tongue while he took her with long, hard thrusts. She was delirious with a pleasure beyond anything she had ever felt. Excitement flamed through her slim body like a ravenous fire that consumed every ounce of energy and thought.

When she felt the urgent tightening at the very centre of her, she sobbed his name. A split second later she was flung from the whirlpool of passion over the edge into rapture. Dizzy and out of control, she tasted ecstasy and abandoned herself to the rippling tremors of shocking delight that seized her. It seemed like for ever before she felt earthbound again.

'Leonidas,' she mumbled, and in that period of quiet joy and respite all her barriers were down. She did what she wanted to do and gave way to the love she kept locked away inside her. She wrapped her arms round him and hugged him tight. She smoothed his damp hair, landed a kiss on just about every part of him within reach and sighed happily in blissful contentment.

Engulfed in that flood-tide of appreciation, Leonidas froze for an instant, and then he almost laughed, for his son was equally affectionate. In a rather abrupt movement for one so graceful, he pressed his lips in a fleeting tribute to the corner of her mouth and rolled free of her. Almost immediately, however, he reached out across the space between them to close a hand over hers. She turned her head and gave him a huge smile.

Familiarity tugged a cord of memory and his ebony brows pleated. 'Do you know? Until this moment I didn't realise that you resemble Imogen, but now I have seen the family likeness.'

'Have you?' Maribel was sharply disconcerted by that unexpected remark and very surprised, as it had never occurred to her that she was in the least like her cousin. Suddenly she felt as if a giant ice cube had settled in the warm pit of her belly and she lay very still and tense.

'It's not obvious,' Leonidas added lazily. 'I think it's more a trick of expression. Your smile reminded me of her.'

Maribel kept on bravely smiling at that news, even though she felt much more like crying. The coolness inside her was spreading like clammy shock through her limbs and chilling her to the bone. In what way could she possibly resemble the late and very beautiful Imogen? She scarcely needed to be told that it could only have been a trick of expression. After all, Imogen had been six inches taller with classic features, long blonde hair and a slender, perfect figure that looked fabulous in even the most unflattering outfit. When Hermione Stratton had pointed out that Maribel could not compare to her late daughter in looks or personality, she had only spoken the truth. Maribel had always accepted that reality. But she was totally devastated when the man she loved told her that she reminded him of Imogen. Had Leonidas slept with her the night that Elias was conceived, purely because of her elusive similarity to her late cousin? In short, had Leonidas been much more attached to Imogen than Maribel had ever been prepared to acknowledge? Slowly, she eased her limp fingers out of his.

A silence stretched that was heavy and long and when the phone buzzed it sounded incredibly loud. Darkness having chasing the gold from his hard gaze, Leonidas sat up in an impatient movement and reached for it. He switched from English to French. 'Josette?'

Maribel also spoke fluent French and she had no trouble working out who the female caller was. Josette Dawnay, the supermodel, was, according to popular report, one of Leonidas' long-term lovers. A gorgeous brunette with reputedly the longest legs on the catwalk, she had most recently accompanied Leonidas to the Cannes film festival. Her risqué reputation had only been heightened by her well-documented loathing of wearing undergarments with the very short skirts that she favoured.

'At your apartment?' Leonidas murmured sibilantly. 'Why not? I won't make it much before ten, though.'

Maribel breathed in so deep, she felt light-headed. It did not clear the leaden sensation of nausea coiled in her sensitive tummy. She scrambled out of bed. She crawled over the floor, got her dress, forced her way into it and stood up, wriggling violently to do up the zip. All the while, Leonidas talked in idiomatic French and watched her with cool dark eyes as though she were the floor show put on to entertain him.

As she straightened and walked round the side of the bed he murmured, 'What *are* you doing now?'

Maribel said nothing. She lifted the water decanter from the cabinet and upended it on his lap.

With a growl of disbelief, Leonidas sprang out of the bed and finished his call. As magnificent naked as a bronzed Greek god, he shook off water and surveyed her with outrage. 'What the hell is this?'

'You've had your deal sweetener and that's as far as it goes. I think you could term this the cooling-off period. If you decide that you still want me to marry you, we need to get one fact straight beforehand,' Maribel breathed with ringing scorn. 'I will not sleep with you while you are sleeping with other women.'

'*Theos mou*…you presume to dictate terms to me?' Leonidas raked at her with sizzling bite.

'Don't be so prejudiced. This could well be the best offer you've ever had, so think long and hard before you refuse it,' Maribel advised, violet eyes flashing with angry warning. 'Let our marriage be platonic and I will ignore your affairs, because I will not consider you to be my husband. Insist on anything more intimate and I will watch your every move and make your life hell if you betray me!'

'Even as my wife, you will not tell me what to do,' Leonidas intoned with all the chilling assurance of his forceful, arrogant character. He stared at her as she reached for the door handle. 'Walk out of this bedroom before morning and I will be angry with you, *hara mou.*'

'Then you're going to be angry.' After listening to that dialogue with Josette Dawnay and having her every worst fear fulfilled, Maribel was too indignant and upset to linger beneath his shrewd scrutiny. 'I'll check on Elias and sleep in one of the other rooms. Goodnight.'

'As you wish.' His lean, darkly handsome face set in forbidding lines of condemnation, Leonidas made no further attempt to dissuade her from leaving.

Maribel went in to see her son, who was slumbering peacefully in his cot. Exchanging a valiant smile with Diane, who had appeared in the doorway of the connecting room, she departed again. She chose a bedroom just across the corridor and closed the door behind her. She felt dead inside, but her mind was going crazy throwing up wounding thoughts and images.

Reality had burst the bubble of her foolish illusions and she felt that she only had herself to blame. Hadn't Leonidas been honest from the outset?

For business arrangement, read marriage of convenience, she thought heavily. He would continue to have his casual mistresses—the stunning, sycophantic tribe of high-profile women who provided him with sexual variety in his travels round the world. Maribel would wear his ring and raise his son and pretend that it didn't matter that she had nothing else. But just then she knew that what she didn't have, what *he* wouldn't give *her*, would matter very, very much to her...

CHAPTER EIGHT

MARIBEL removed a petal from the flower. 'I love him.' That petal dropped like a little stone to the gravel below the stone seat. 'I hate him,' she breathed and several petals came off in unison and fluttered further afield in the breeze that was blowing across the rose garden. Mouse and Elias scampered past her, chasing along the elaborate maze of box-hedged paths with noisy enjoyment. Maribel ended her idle game with the flower on a note of hatred that made her superstitiously tear that final petal in half before she cast the stem aside.

Nobody needed to tell Maribel that hatred was the dark side of love, but she could not have told a soul at the moment what was in her heart. Yet her wedding day was fast approaching. The event had been so pumped up by press speculation and excitement that she had been forced to take advantage of the privacy on offer at Heyward Park. At his father's country house, Elias could at least play without the threat of a camera lens suddenly zooming out of the shrubbery. The level of curiosity about the most junior member of the Pallis family was alarmingly strong.

Maribel was also virtually homeless since an attempted break-in at the empty farmhouse had left her with no

choice but to agree to the removal of all her personal possessions. The university term had ended and she had
cleared out her desk after handing in her notice. She was
shaken by the speed at which her comfortable, quiet and
secure life had been dismantled. Indeed, the pace of change
engulfing her had left her more than a little shell-shocked
and she was feeling the strain.

In just three days' time it would be too late to back out
of becoming a Pallis, Maribel reflected fearfully. It was
most unlike her, and she had never been a coward, but sometimes she just felt like scooping up Elias and running for
her life. She covered her face with cool hands and breathed
in slow and deep. She couldn't do that to Leonidas; she
couldn't jilt him at the altar just because she was absolutely
terrified that she might be making a very big mistake. He
was so proud, he would never get over the insult. In any
case, everything was organised to the nth degree, right down
to the fabulous designer wedding dress and a string of little
Greek flower-girls and page-boys selected from Leonidas'
extended family circle. Under pressure, Ginny had agreed
to act as her matron of honour, and Maribel had felt forced
to accept the offer of Imogen's sisters, Amanda and Agatha,
as bridesmaids. They were the only family she had left. Had
she snubbed them, it would probably have caused embarrassing comment in the local papers and she knew she owed
her aunt and uncle more than that.

Ginny had accurately forecast how association with a
billionaire might affect the people around Maribel. No
sooner had word of the engagement been made public
than the Strattons had landed *en bloc* on Maribel's doorstep
to mend fences. Her aunt had thought better of cutting off
all contact with a niece on the brink of marrying one of the

richest men in the world. But the Stratton family had
decided to acknowledge Elias somewhat too late in the day
to impress Maribel and she had felt horribly uncomfortable with such a calculating parade of insincerity.

Her state of mind had not been helped by the fact that
she had scarcely seen Leonidas. Since their mutually dis-
satisfied parting before his trip to New York, Leonidas had
been colder than ice. He had spent most of the interven-
ing weeks abroad and had only returned to the UK twice
for fleeting visits to see Elias. She did not flatter herself
that a desire to see her had figured on his agenda. His
scrupulous politeness and reserve had warned her that
marriage promised to be an even bigger challenge than she
had feared, for he had the resistance of granite towards any
attempt to change him. But, on balance, she did know that
he very definitely wanted the wedding to go ahead. How
did she know that? Well, certainly not by anything he had
said, Maribel conceded ruefully.

Every day, Maribel had scoured every magazine and
newspaper and had failed to find a single photo of Leonidas
with another woman. This was so highly unusual that she
could not believe it was a coincidence. For the first time
in his notoriously racy existence, Leonidas appeared to be
embracing a low social profile. Even the gossip columns
were commenting on his new discreet lifestyle and laying
bets as to how long it would last. But Maribel could have
given them the answer to that question: until *after* the
wedding.

It was her belief that Leonidas had decided not to rock
the boat until they were safely married and he had finally
acquired equal rights over the son he loved. That was surely
why he had made the effort to phone her every day. He had

also sent her gifts so lavish they took her breath away. On the phone he talked about Elias and did not deviate, even if she tried to throw in a tripwire. Anything more exciting than the weather got him off the phone fast, which she found counter-productive because even when she was furious with him she liked listening to the sound of his voice.

On the gift front, however, she was doing very nicely indeed, and had riches been her sole motivation she would have been ecstatic and ready to sprint down the aisle. To date, she had acquired designer handbags, sunglasses, a watch, a fancy phone, fabulous luggage, a diamond pendant, a superb pearl necklace and matching earrings, two paintings, a sculpture, a jewelled collar for Mouse, a Mercedes car—with the promise of a personalised version to arrive in the near future—the latest books, sundry female outfits that caught his eye. No, Leonidas was not afraid to shop. And so it went on: the gift-giving that she saw as a substitute for what he would not or could not say. To be fair to him, he was very generous, but he was also accustomed to buying loyalty, soothing wounded feelings and pleasing people with the spoils of his wealth. Spending money cost him a lot less effort than other, more lasting and demanding responses.

After all, Leonidas knew why she was angry with him, but he had yet to make the smallest attempt to explain himself or set her fears to rest. The evening she had known he would be with Josette Dawnay, Mirabel had lain awake all night in an absolute torment of anger, jealousy and hatred. She had tortured herself by surfing the net to scrutinise photos of the gorgeous model. A kind of terror of the future had gripped her when she had appreciated that if she married Leonidas and he insisted on his freedom, the torture she was undergoing would just go on and on and on with a series of different faces in the role of rival. Only, how could any normal woman even consider trying to compete with such fantastically beautiful women?

'Dr Greenaway? You have a visitor.' A staff member appeared at the entrance to the rose garden and Maribel stood up in haste, since any distraction from her troubled thoughts was welcome. 'Princess Hussein Al-Zafar is waiting in the drawing room.'

For a moment, Maribel was confused by the impressive title and then a huge smile chased the tension from her soft mouth. Pausing only to gather up Elias and Mouse, she headed back into the mansion at speed. Tilda Crawford! Tilda and her husband, Crown Prince Rashad of Bakhar, had been the only names that appeared on both bride and groom's guest lists. Maribel had been relieved and delighted when she had received an acceptance. Although Rashad remained one of Leonidas' closest friends from his university days, Maribel was aware that Tilda and Leonidas had only ever mixed like oil and water.

Maribel and Tilda had met when Tilda had come to one of Imogen's parties and taken instant refuge in the kitchen when Leonidas had walked in. 'Sorry, I can't stand that Pallis guy,' Tilda confided flatly. 'I once dated a friend of his and, because I worked as a waitress, Leonidas treated me like a gold-digging tart.'

Maribel had found that indifference to Leonidas' status, spectacular good looks and wealth extremely attractive, and she and Tilda had become friends. Since Tilda had married her prince, however, and settled into royal family life abroad, the two women had had little contact. Maribel was guiltily aware that she was partially responsible for that, because the prospect of having to tell Tilda that Leonidas was her son's father had seriously embarrassed her.

'Tilda!' Maribel smiled warmly at the stunningly lovely blonde woman awaiting her arrival. She had paused only to see Mouse into his hidey-hole below the hall table—placed there for that purpose—and hand Elias over to the attentions of his nanny.

Turquoise-blue eyes sparkling, the princess moved forward to greet her. 'Maribel—it's wonderful to see you again.'

'Oh, my goodness, I suppose I should've curtsied, or something. I quite forgot your royal status!' Maribel grasped Tilda's outstretched hands and gave them an affectionate squeeze.

'Don't be silly. That stuff is only for public occasions,' Tilda scolded. 'Is …er…Leonidas here?'

Aware of the other woman's tension, Maribel was quick to reassure her. 'No. You're safe. Leonidas is still abroad.'

Tilda gave her a guilty look of apology. 'Is it so obvious that I want to avoid him? I'm sorry—how horribly rude I'm being!'

'You and he never hit it off. Don't let that come between us,' Maribel told her with complete calm. 'Now how long can you stay for? We have so much to catch up on.'

A tray of tea and delicate little nibbles was brought in and served.

'I was really disappointed that I couldn't come to your wedding in Bakhar,' Maribel confided. 'It wasn't possible for me to leave Imogen at the time. She wasn't well at all.'

'I understood that. You were amazingly patient with her.'

'I was very fond of Imogen.' Even so, ever since Leonidas had confided that Maribel reminded him of

Imogen, Maribel's self-esteem had nosedived. She was crushed by the conviction that she had only ever been a poor substitute for her cousin, and haunted by the suspicion that she had no right whatsoever to expect or ask for anything more than tolerance and acceptance from Leonidas. Surely if she had been the morally decent woman she liked to believe she was, she would have withstood the temptation that Leonidas had offered on the night that Elias was conceived?

'I saw your son walking into the house with you,' the princess remarked softly. 'He looks very like Leonidas.'

'I imagine you were very shocked to find out who his father was.'

Tilda looked troubled. 'How frank can I be?'

'Totally frank.'

'I was very concerned.' Tilda pulled a face and her voice became hesitant. 'I'm probably about to offend you for ever when I tell you why I felt I had to come and see you before your wedding.'

'I doubt that very much. I don't take offence easily, especially not with the people I trust.'

'I was afraid that you might feel you have no choice but to marry Leonidas to retain custody of your son. He's a formidable man and very powerful.' Tilda released her breath in an anxious sigh. 'But you *do* have a choice—I'm willing to offer you financial backing if you need it to go through the courts and fight him.'

'Does Rashad know about this?'

Tilda frowned. 'Rashad and Leonidas have a friendship quite independent of our marriage. I'll be honest— Rashad wouldn't approve of my interference, particularly when there is a child involved, but I have my own money and my own convictions about what's right and what's wrong.'

'You're a dear friend.' Maribel was very much touched by Tilda's offer of monetary assistance. 'But I'm going to marry Leonidas. I could give you a whole host of reasons why. Yes, I do feel under pressure. I do feel I can't compete. But at the same time, Leonidas is wonderful with Elias and my son needs a father more than I wanted to admit.'

'There's more to marriage than raising children,' Tilda said wryly.

A rueful smile touched Maribel's lips and for the first time in weeks she felt curiously at peace with the turmoil of her emotions, because one unchanging truth sat at the centre of it all. 'I've always loved Leonidas, Tilda—even when he was the most unlovable guy around. I can't even explain why. It's been that way almost since the first time I saw him.'

Leonidas returned to Heyward Park late the night before the wedding. He flew in from Greece with a plane-load of relatives. Mirabel chose a classic top and skirt in russet shades to wear with the pearl necklace and earrings, and greeted the arrivals in the front hall. Leonidas entered last, just in time to overhear his bride-to-be chatting quite comfortably with his trio of great-aunts, not one of whom spoke a word of English. Her grasp of Greek was basic but more than adequate for the occasion. A light supper was on offer, but there was also provision for the less lively members of his family who preferred to retire for the night in readiness for the celebrations the next day. Her confidence in dealing with both staff and guests was impressive. But he was quick to notice that her lush curves had slimmed down, and that when she saw him her clear eyes screened and her delicate features tightened.

'My apologies for bringing a large party back at this hour, *glikia mou*,' Leonidas murmured. 'And my compliments for handling them with so much grace and charm.'

'Thanks.' Her acknowledgement of compliments from a most unusual source was brisk. Even a brief encounter with his brilliant dark eyes was sufficient to raise self-conscious colour in her cheeks. She could greet his sixty-odd relatives with equanimity, but one glimpse of him reduced her to a schoolgirlish discomfiture that mortified her. With his stylishly cut ebony hair and lean, sculpted bone structure he looked devastatingly handsome. His black business suit was perfectly tailored to his lithe powerful frame. As usual, he emanated high-voltage masculinity and rampant sex appeal.

Curving a casual arm to her spine to draw her to one side, Leonidas inclined his arrogant dark head. 'When did you start learning Greek?'

'Soon after Elias was born, but I haven't always had the time I would like to concentrate on it.' Although the contact between them was of the slightest, Maribel was as stiff as a stick of rock. 'Excuse me, your great-aunts are waiting for me. I promised to show them some photos of Elias.'

'Don't I have priority?' Astonished at being treated in such an offhand manner, Leonidas closed a staying hand over hers before she could walk away.

Maribel was achingly conscious of the compelling force of his dark golden eyes. He possessed an intense charisma that she could not withstand even when she was angry with him. Her heart was beating very fast. 'Of course,' she said very politely.

The distance Leonidas sensed in her was like a wall. He didn't like it. He had assumed that the passage of time would take care of that problem and he had been wrong. Raw frustration raked through him. He thought of all the women in the past and the present who would have done anything he wanted, who would not have dreamt of angering him or criticising him. Or of making demands he was unwilling to meet. And finally he thought of Maribel who was just…Maribel, and unique. Her ability to wage a war of passive resistance was driving him crazy.

'Tomorrow is our wedding day. In the light of that fact,' Leonidas drawled with sardonic bite, 'I will explain to you that Josette Dawnay has opened an art gallery in the same building as her apartment and I was invited to the opening, along with a lot of other people. If you feel the need to check the date, you should find ample evidence of those facts.'

A tide of guilty pink flushed Maribel's creamy complexion. Relief leapt through her, but it was tinged by a streak of defiance, for she could not see why he could not have laid her concerns to rest at the time. 'I suppose I should say that I'm sorry I drenched you—'

'You should,' Leonidas confirmed without hesitation.

'I'm sorry, but you could have explained.'

'Why should I have? You eavesdropped on a private conversation and jumped to the wrong conclusion,' Leonidas countered with a sibilant cool that was a challenge. 'How was that my fault?'

Maribel was continually amazed at the ease with which Leonidas could infuriate her. He had buckets of unapologetic attitude. Aggressive, dynamic, intensely competitive, he was a living, breathing testament to the power of testosterone. She could feel the eyes of their guests lingering on them. It was one of those times when walking away seemed the wisest option. 'Excuse me,' she murmured again and off she went.

If Leonidas had been astonished by her attitude just minutes earlier, he was even more stunned by this resolute retreat. For the first time in his life, he had made a conciliatory move towards a woman and what was his reward? Where were the abject apologies and the passionate appreciation he had expected to receive? Something touched the toe of his shoe. Eyes smouldering, he glanced down. Mouse had crawled out from below his table. Shaking with nerves at the number of strangers about him, the wolfhound had nonetheless battled his terror to finally sneak out far enough from cover to welcome Leonidas home. Leonidas bent down and patted the shaggy head for that much-appreciated demonstration of loyalty.

Having ensured that all the guests had had their needs attended to, Maribel wasted no time in going straight up to bed. She thought of what Leonidas had told her. All her heartache over Josette Dawnay had been needless, a storm in a teacup that Leonidas could have settled in seconds— had he so desired. That he had not chosen to do so sent her a message, one she would have sooner not received. Leonidas had declared his independence and his freedom. He had spelt out the fact that marriage wasn't going to change his lifestyle.

Her eyes prickled in the darkness. She drew in a deep sustaining breath and scolded herself for being too emotional. She had to learn how to make the best of things, not just for her own sanity but for her son's sake as well. Tomorrow was her wedding day, she reminded herself doggedly. So many people had gone to so much trouble to ensure that every detail would be perfect—the very least she could do was try to enjoy it.

Shortly before six o'clock the next morning, Leonidas was wakened by a phone call from Vasos. Five minutes later, Leonidas was studying tabloid headlines on a computer screen and swearing eloquently in Greek. He raked his sleep-tousled black hair off his brow. PALLIS STAG CRUISE…RIOTOUS REVELRY WITH EXOTIC DANCERS! He flicked on to another page. It only got worse. The photos made him groan out loud in disbelief.

'Who the hell took these pictures?'

Vasos stepped forward. 'Camera phone…one of the dancers Sergio Torrente brought on board for the party. Crude, but effective.'

'Thank you, Sergio,' Leonidas breathed rawly.

Forty-eight hours earlier, his friend, Sergio Torrente, had mustered a crowd of male friends and staged a surprise stag party on his yacht for Leonidas' benefit. Sergio, who loathed weddings, was now safe deep in the jungles of Borneo on one of the Action-Man trips he enjoyed, well away from the furore he had unleashed on the bridegroom.

'I've taken the liberty of removing the daily newspapers from the house,' Vasos admitted.

Dismissing Vasos, Leonidas snapped shut the laptop. He knew Vasos could only be trying to protect Maribel, since nothing shocked the Pallis family. In five hours time, he was getting married. Or was he? Strategic planning and self-preservation came naturally to Leonidas. A business-man to the backbone, he had the Machiavellian genes of a family that had been merchant bankers in the Middle Ages. While over-indulgence in the sins of the flesh had proved the downfall of previous generations of the Pallis family, Leonidas was a great deal more grounded than most people appreciated.

But although plotting and planning were the spice of life to him, he was uneasily aware that Maribel had an intolerant view of such tactics. But would she still go ahead and marry him if she got the chance to read that tabloid trash? How much faith did she have in him? *None*, came the answer. Maribel didn't even pretend to have faith in him. Overhearing a single ambiguous phone call had been sufficient to make her judge and condemn him out of hand.

Leonidas brooded over the problem and, in the interests of fairness, felt duty-bound to ask himself why Maribel *should* trust him. The past three weeks replayed at supersonic speed in his mind. His strong, blue-shadowed jawline squared. Last night he had noticed that she had lost weight. He knew that stress was the most likely cause. She had loved her job and her home and she'd had to surrender both at short notice. Maybe she had been fond of the boyfriend, as well, Leonidas allowed grudgingly. He hadn't wanted to know the details, so he hadn't asked. She had once accused him of only ever doing what he wanted to do and, in this case, he recognised the accuracy of the charge. He had held onto his anger and punished her for daring to stand up to him. He had abandoned her to sink or swim in a world that was very new to her and she was naturally showing signs of strain.

Another woman might have asked him for support, but not Maribel. No, not Maribel, who was as stubborn as he was. Obstinacy was not a good trait for them to share, Leonidas acknowledged, his wide, sensual mouth compressed. A single request for advice or assistance, one little hint that she regretted challenging him, and all would have been well. Generosity in victory was not a problem for him. Unfortunately, Maribel refused to admit defeat. He was beginning to grasp how Maribel could once have said that she didn't like him. That statement had stayed with him in a nagging memory of unpleasantness that he could not forget. But now he had to ask himself: what was to like? He had been callous and cold towards her. He had been absent when he should have been present. And, in refusing to give her a shred of reassurance, he had simply increased her distrust.

Maribel might be as tranquil as a woodland pool on the surface, but she could be amazingly passionate and hasty, he reminded himself grimly. She was a firecracker, who tended to shoot first and ask questions second. That was not a confidence-boosting attribute on the day that he needed her to go to the altar and say yes with a smile. He had already grasped the reality that, in her eyes, he would always be guilty until proven innocent. A refreshing change after a lifetime of women who were too careful to ask loaded questions or make rash demands.

As the hazy morning mist slowly lifted back to reveal the lush green of the immaculately kept grounds and the promise of the glorious summer day yet to come Leonidas reached a decision. He would tell her about the stag-doe fiasco *after* the wedding. A wedding was a once-in-a-lifetime event, and nothing should be allowed to cast a cloud over Maribel's day. Or give her good reason to decide that marrying him might not be in her best interests.

CHAPTER NINE

'REALITY-CHECK here!' Ginny made a comic show of pinching herself while gaping at the dazzling contents of the sumptuous leather case that Maribel had opened. 'A diamond tiara fit for a queen to wear! That will look amazing with your veil.'

'It would look amazing with anything,' Maribel pointed out dry-mouthed, touching the glittering sapphire and diamond jewels with a reverent fingertip. 'But don't you think it might be a touch over-the-top?'

'Maribel…conspicuous consumption goes hand in hand with being a Pallis. The eight hundred guests will expect lots of bling, and most of them will be wearing their jewels.'

Later that morning, finally free of the combined attentions of the hair stylist, the beautician, the manicurist and the make-up artist, Maribel examined her unfamiliar reflection in the bedroom mirror. She was secretly enthralled by her appearance. Every day of her adult life she had played safe with fashion until she'd fallen madly in love with a bold eighteenth-century-style gown in a bridal portfolio. The boned and piped corset top accentuated her tiny waist before flaring out into a glorious full crackling skirt.

Fashioned in rich gold taffeta and silk, it was a wonderfully glamorous dress. The tiara looked superb anchored
in the glossy chestnut coils of her upswept hair with a
gossamer-fine French lace veil caught at the back of her
head.

The church, a substantial building in weathered stone,
was on the Heyward Park estate. Its private entrance, allied
to the heavy security and a police presence, ensured that
the paparazzi could not get closer than the road that lay
beyond the solid hedge.

'I admire your calm so much,' her cousin, Amanda
Stratton, remarked sweetly, while Ginny and several
parents coaxed the enchantingly pretty flower- girls and the
lively little page-boys into matching pairs. 'As Mummy
says, nine out of ten women would be threatening to leave
Leonidas Pallis standing at the altar.'

Maribel frowned. 'Why would I do something like
that?'

Ginny Bell leant closer to Amanda Stratton and said
something. The pretty blonde went red and stalked off.

'What was she getting at?' Mirabel asked her friend in
an urgent undertone.

'Maybe the rumour that Leonidas is marrying you
without even the safety net of a prenuptial agreement was
more than she could bear. Or, maybe it's the sight of your
diamonds. Whatever, its source is the sour grapes of envy
and you shouldn't pay the slightest heed to it,' the older
woman told her roundly.

Maribel felt as though she had just received a very
sensible piece of advice. The sinking spirits she had
suffered before midnight had been raised by her natural
energy and optimism. Her marriage, she reflected, would

be what she made of it. She breathed in deep as the doors were opened and the sweet mellow notes of organ music swelled out into the vestibule. The scent of the massed roses in the church hung heavy on the air.

Leonidas had nerves as strong as steel, but he had not enjoyed the most soothing start to the day and matters had only got worse. He had spent the morning in a disturbing state of indecision unlike anything he had ever experienced. Aware that his supposed stag cruise exploits might well feature on certain television news channels and on various celebrity websites, he had wondered what he would do if Maribel accessed either before she left for the church. On no less than three occasions he had reached the conclusion that he should move fast and give her his version of events first, only to change his mind again.

'The bride has arrived,' his best man, Prince Rashad, delivered in an aside, quietly marvelling at his friend's perceptible tension and unease, and wondering if he was witnessing the reaction of a reluctant bridegroom. It was true that Maribel was a comfortable ten minutes late, but Rashad found it hard to credit that Leonidas could have feared that his wife-to-be might not turn up.

Leonidas swung right round to check that information out firsthand. And there was Maribel, exotic and vibrant in rustling gold-and-white taffeta that provided a superlative frame for her smooth creamy skin and chestnut hair. She lit up the church in a vivid splash of colour and he was so entranced he forgot to turn back again to face the altar in time-honoured tradition.

'Mummy!' It was Elias, who broke the spell by wriggling off his nanny's lap with the speed and energy of an electric eel to hurl himself in Maribel's direction.

Leonidas strode forward to intercept his son and he hoisted the little boy high before he could trip the bride or her attendants up. Laughter and smiles broke out amongst their guests.

Maribel's attention locked to Leonidas and refused to budge. In tails and pinstripe trousers matched with a stylish cravat that toned with her dress, he would have made any woman stare. She met his stunning dark golden eyes and it was as if the rest of the world, and certainly everyone in the church, had vanished in a puff of smoke. All she was aware of was Leonidas. A sweet, wanton tide of warmth slivered silken fingers of anticipation through her slim frame.

Ginny took Elias from Leonidas. Leonidas grasped Maribel's fingers and bent his darkly handsome head to press a kiss to the delicate blue-veined skin of her inner wrist. It was more of a caress than a kiss and, although that contact only lasted for an instant, it sent a tingling sensual message to her every nerve-ending and left her trembling.

She was afraid to look at him again during the service in case she forgot where she was again. Yet she remained aware of him with every fibre of her being. She gave her responses in a clear voice that sounded a lot calmer than she felt. They exchanged rings. Her tension eased the moment they were pronounced man and wife. He retained his hold on her hand.

'You look magnificent, *hara mou*,' Leonidas told her huskily. 'That colour was made for you.'

'I was terrified I would look as if I was starring in a costume drama,' Maribel whispered back, encouraged into a burst of confidence. 'But I just fell totally for the dress.'

'You were rather late arriving at the church.' Leonidas reached down to lift Elias, who was resisting his nanny's attempt to remove him from the midst of things. Tired and fed up with being cooed over and admired, the little boy was starting to get cross.

'It's traditional.' Maribel laughed, touched and pleased by the way Leonidas was beginning to intuitively look out for his son even when Elias was in a less-than appealing mood. 'I could hardly leave you with all that luggage monogrammed with my new married initials.'

Leonidas discovered that his sense of humour wasn't quite as robust as usual. He had a disconcerting vision of those suitcases piled up with all the other gifts he had given her. It would be like Maribel to leave every present behind if she left him. It bothered him that he still felt that edgy. A wedding ring would make any woman stop and think before doing anything foolish or impulsive, wouldn't it? She was a church-goer and she had taken vows and made promises. Even so, all of a sudden, he was wondering at what precise point a marriage became official and binding—before or after the consummation?

In the vehicle that carried them back very slowly to the house, Maribel felt a little uncomfortable with her bride-groom's silence. 'How do you feel now that you've "got it all over with"?' she asked, striving for a light teasing note because she was hoping to receive an answer that would soothe her insecurities.

'*Relieved,*' Leonidas admitted with the emphasis of pure sincerity, although he felt he would be even more relieved when the day was over. He was making a valiant effort to rise above the ignominy of being forced to travel in an open carriage lined with blue velvet and drawn by four white horses prancing along with azure plumes bobbing in their head collars. He was learning a lot about Maribel's bridal preferences and a great deal of it was surprisingly colourful stuff, wholly out of step with her bridegroom's sophisticated tastes.

Maribel felt that, had they just attended a very trying event, she could have understood if he had confessed to a sense of relief. Just as quickly, she scolded herself for being oversensitive. Many men were reputed to dislike the fuss and formality of weddings. Was she getting carried away with the fantasy of her theatrical dress, the church romantically awash with roses, or the thrill of the carriage ride? She gave herself a stern lecture, because a magical wedding day didn't really change anything. It didn't mean that Leonidas would be miraculously transformed into a guy who loved her as much as she loved him. That was the stuff of dreams and she was a practical woman, wasn't she?

When the carriage drew up outside the house, Leonidas sprang out with alacrity and reached up to lift his bride down. But he didn't put her down again. Black lashes curling low over mesmeric golden eyes, he prised her lips apart with a sensual flick of his tongue and set about plundering the delicate interior of her mouth with a carnal expertise that caught her wholly unprepared. Her mind went blank; she was overwhelmed. Sensual firecrackers of response went fizzing and flaring through her bloodstream. The tips of her breasts tingled and her insides turned liquid. Slowly he lowered her again until her fancy golden shoes found purchase on the plush red carpet that ran up to the entrance doors.

Eyes like sapphire stars, Maribel parted her love-bruised lips. She was about to speak when a movement to one side

of Leonidas attracted her attention. The sight of a stranger
with a camera, signalling her to stay still for another
moment, rocked her back to planet earth again with a jarring
thump. She had neither noticed nor recalled the team of pro-
fessionals engaged to film their wedding day for posterity.
But Leonidas was a good deal more observant. With perfect
timing he had just delivered a perfectly choreographed
clinch to mark the bridal couple's arrival at the house.

'*Gone with the Wind* has got nothing on you,' Maribel
remarked in a brittle voice, mortified pink highlighting her
cheekbones. 'Well, you did promise to ensure a good
surface show and that was very much in line with what's
expected of a bridegroom.'

Leonidas wondered when she had developed the atro-
cious habit of remembering everything he had ever said
and tossing it back to him like a log on a fire when he didn't
feel like a blaze. 'That's not why I kissed you, *hara mou*.'

'Isn't it?'

'No. It is not,' Leonidas framed with succinct bite.

Maribel tossed her head as much as she dared, for she
did not want to dislodge her tiara. 'Well, I don't believe you.'

'Why don't we leave our guests to party alone and head
straight to the bedroom right now, *mali mou*?' Leonidas
intoned that offer in the softest, silkiest voice imaginable.
'I'm ready and willing. Would you believe me then? Would
that prove that sexual hunger rather than a wish to pose for
the camera-lens powered me?'

Violet-blue eyes wide, her heart thudding at the foot of
her throat with shock, Maribel stared up at him aghast.
Dangerous dark, deep-set eyes glittered down at her in a
ruthless challenge that was all rogue male laced with
white-hot sexuality. Her mouth ran dry, for she knew in-

stantly that he wasn't playing games. Indeed she had a horrible suspicion that abandoning their guests and all the hoopla that would go with entertaining them was a prospect that held considerable attraction for Leonidas.

'Yes, it would…er…but I really don't think that we need go that far,' she muttered hurriedly.

'No?' His entire attention was welded to her. Not by so much as a flicker did he betray any awareness of the staff assembled on the far side of the hall to greet them or of the long procession of limousines pulling up outside to disgorge the first guests.

'No,' she whispered unevenly.

Leonidas stroked a blunt brown forefinger across the flush of colour illuminating her creamy complexion. 'No?' he queried thickly. 'Even if it's what I want most in the world at this moment, *hara mou*?'

Her heart was racing. Her breath had snarled up in her throat. His dark, rich drawl, his brilliant, provocative gaze, controlled her. She could feel the wild heat in him igniting a flame low in her pelvis and her legs quivered under her. *Don't I get priority?* he had asked the night before. Suddenly she wanted to give him that priority, no matter what the cost.

'Okay…if that's what you want,' she heard herself say in capitulation, and could then scarcely believe that she had said it.

Surprise and appreciation flashed through Leonidas. At last, *yes*. The strength of his satisfaction astonished him. She was so conventional, so careful. He knew the worth of his triumph and the power of his appeal. Golden eyes smouldering, he grasped her hand and carried her slender fingers to his lips with a gentleness that was rare for him.

'Thank you, *kardoula mou*. But I won't embarrass you like that.'

Disappointment and relief gripped Maribel in equal parts. But people were joining them; introductions had to be made, good wishes and congratulations received. The bustling busyness of being a hostess as well as a bride took over for Maribel, who had gently refused her aunt's suggestion that she take charge for her niece's benefit. When Maribel got her first free moment, she devoted it to Elias, who needed a cuddle and a little time alone with his mother before he would settle down for a long-overdue nap.

She was taking a short cut from the nursery down a rear staircase to the ballroom when she heard a name and a familiar giggle that made her pause.

'Of course, if Imogen had lived,' her cousin Amanda was saying with authority while she fussed with her hair in front of a gilded mirror, 'Maribel would never have got near Leonidas. Imogen was gorgeous and she would never have popped a sprog just to get a guy to the altar.'

'Do you really think Maribel planned her pregnancy?'

'Of course, she did. It must've been right after the funeral—Maribel pounced when Leonidas was drunk, or something…I mean, he *must* have been drunk and upset about my sister!'

Praying that she would not have to suffer the ultimate humiliation of being seen, Maribel began to tiptoe back up the stairs. Unfortunately Amanda's shrill voice carried with clarity after her.

'Imogen thought it was so hilarious that Maribel had the hots for Leonidas that she told him. But I don't suppose my sister would be laughing if she were here today. Did you see that tiara? Did you see the size of those diamonds?

And what does Maribel do to say thank you? She sticks her billionaire in a tacky carriage drawn by horses that looked like they came straight out of a circus!'

Maribel headed for the main staircase at the other side of the great house. Her tummy was knotted with nausea. Had the carriage idea been tacky? How naïve of her not to appreciate that their sudden marriage would create loads of unpleasant rumours! How could anyone think that she had *planned* to fall pregnant? But perhaps this was a shotgun wedding in the sense that she had put Leonidas under pressure with regard to their son. So what right had she to be so thin-skinned?

Some of the comments, however, cut even deeper and hurt much more. Had she taken advantage of the fact that Leonidas was grieving the night after the funeral? They had both been grieving. Even so, that suggestion hit a very sensitive spot. She was still afraid that the only reason Leonidas had gone to bed with her in the first place was that she had reminded him of Imogen. And could it be true that Imogen had guessed how Maribel felt about Leonidas and told him? Made Maribel the butt of a joke? Her cousin, she recalled painfully, had had a rather cruel sense of humour that many people had enjoyed. And none more so, in those far-off student days, than Leonidas. She was cringing at the idea that he might know her biggest secret, might always have known. *Eavesdroppers never heard good of themselves.* She wondered who was responsible for that irrelevant old chestnut. She felt absolutely gutted.

The instant Maribel returned to Leonidas' side, he noticed that something was wrong. Her inner glow had dimmed; her sparkle had dulled. When the meal was served, her healthy appetite had vanished and she picked at her food and evaded his gaze. His tension increased. He knew it had been a big mistake to let her out of his sight. Someone had referred to the stag party and she was upset. He was convinced, however, that she was too well mannered to confront him in public. As he sat there brooding on how best to handle the fallout the appeal of the Italian honeymoon he had organised began to steadily recede. His Tuscan palazzo was exquisite, but there would be airports within reasonable reach as well as towns with easy transport links. Although he always travelled with his own staff, it would be hard to keep the lid on any major marital breakdown. If Maribel decided to be especially lacking in understanding and forgiveness, she would find it all too easy to walk out on him in Italy.

Having reached the conclusion that he might easily live to regret a Tuscan honeymoon, Leonidas decided to take his bride straight back home to the island of Zelos, where he had been born. Surrounded by sea and an army of devoted retainers, Maribel would not be going anywhere in a hurry, or without his consent. He would have all the time in the world to dissuade her from making any hasty or unwise decisions. Inclining his arrogant dark head to signal Vasos over to him, Leonidas communicated his change of heart.

Only when he had done that did he consider the reality that he was making plans to virtually imprison his wife. A very slight frisson of unease assailed Leonidas at that acknowledgement. When he studied Maribel's pale delicate profile, his core of inner steel held him steady. Look what had happened the last time he had given her the freedom to make her own choices! She had only gone through a pregnancy alone and unprotected! A pregnancy with *his* child, which he should have shared in right from the start, Leonidas reasoned fiercely. When she made bad decisions like that, it was hardly surprising that he should feel the need to take control. In any case even Stone Age Man had known it was his duty to protect the family unit.

Tilda insisted on accompanying Maribel when she went upstairs to get changed. 'I owe you an apology for misjudging Leonidas,' the beautiful blonde murmured with twinkling turquoise eyes. 'Just like the rest of us, he has matured and changed since he was at uni.'

Maribel cast off her private worries to summon up a warm smile that put Tilda at her ease. 'And what brought on that realisation?'

'Apart from the fact that he has been really charming to me today? When I see Leonidas with you and Elias, he is a very different guy from the one I remember,' the princess confessed. 'And while I was astonished when I learned that you and he were a couple, my husband wasn't. He said that you were the only woman Leonidas ever sought out for an intelligent conversation.'

Maribel nodded, but felt just then that intelligent conversation wasn't a lot to offer to one of the world's most notorious womanisers.

'Is there something worrying you?' Tilda asked gently. 'Is it all that stag cruise nonsense?'

Maribel veiled her startled eyes before she could betray her ignorance on that subject. She concentrated on donning a turquoise and pink dress that was both elegant and comfortable to travel in. 'Er…no.'

'I knew you would be too sensible to let anything of that

nature bother you. After all, men will be men, and our men in particular will always be paparazzi targets,' Tilda remarked wryly. 'Rashad would have been on that yacht with Sergio and Leonidas, if he hadn't had to take my father-in-law's place at a government meeting.'

Stag-cruise nonsense? Don't go there, Maribel told herself staunchly. None of her business, was it? So soon after that unfortunate misunderstanding over Josette Dawnay, Maribel was in no hurry to suspect the worst. In any case, she was still too much taken up with tormenting herself with the suspicion that Leonidas might always have known that she loved him. She really couldn't bear that idea, she really could *not* live with that possibility, she acknowledged tautly. Without her pride she felt she would have nothing.

Maribel studied the island far below them as the helicopter wheeled round in a turn. There was just enough light left for her to get a good view. Zelos was surprisingly lush and green and there were loads of trees. Long slices of golden sand were edged by the turquoise of the sea that washed the shores. She thought it looked like paradise. A very substantial residence occupied a magnificent site in splendid isolation at one end of the island. At the other, there was a picturesque fishing village with a church and a huge yacht in the harbour. Zelos was where Leonidas had grown up and, for that reason alone, she was fascinated by the prospect of living on the island.

Darkness had fallen when Elias was welcomed into the big sprawling house as though he were royalty. Maribel watched her son being borne off to bed by Diane and her co-nanny, a young Greek woman, closely followed by the housekeeper, the nursery maids and her son's personal protection officer. Slowly she shook her head. 'Elias is never going to be alone again, is he?'

'We Greeks are gregarious by nature. I was alone too much as a child but, just as I was, he will be watched over by everyone on the island. Welcome to your new home, *hara mou*.' Leonidas closed a shapely brown hand over hers. 'Let me show you the house.'

It was as large as Heyward Park, for several generations of his family had built new wings to suit their individual tastes. In a glorious room that opened out onto a beautiful vine-shaded terrace, Leonidas tugged her into his arms with immense care.

'I want you to be happy here,' he told her huskily.

Maribel stared up into his brilliant dark eyes and felt her heart lurch. She had promised herself that she would not stoop to asking Leonidas any foolish questions. But suddenly she could no longer withstand her need to know the truth. 'There's something I want to ask you, Leonidas,' she breathed abruptly.

Leonidas regarded her in level enquiry.

'Did Imogen tell you years ago that I was in love with you?' Maribel completed.

It was the very last question that Leonidas could have foreseen. Having braced himself for a query of an entirely different nature, indeed an accusation, he was bemused.

Maribel stepped out of his loosened hold. 'It's true. She *did* tell you!'

Leonidas frowned. 'You haven't even given me the chance to answer you.'

Maribel drew herself up to her full height. 'You don't need to. Sometimes I can read you like a book.'

Leonidas was anything but reassured by that statement. He had long regarded his famed impassivity as a source of privacy that he could take for granted. Once or twice before, however, she had given him cause to suspect that she did possess a certain rare insight where he was concerned. 'Imogen might once have mentioned something of that nature,' he conceded with the utmost casualness.

'Well, it's not something you need to worry about,' Maribel told him firmly.

'I wasn't worrying.'

'Or think about.'

'I wasn't thinking about it either.'

'Because it's no longer true,' Maribel informed him doggedly, keen to get any such notion knocked right back out of his handsome head again. 'I got over you after that night at Imogen's house.'

His superb bone structure tightened beneath his bronzed skin. 'Why?'

Over two years of pent-up hostility and hurt were suddenly rising up inside Maribel in an unfettered overflow of feelings. 'You remember you asked for breakfast? There was no food in the house, so I—fool that I was—I went out to buy some.'

Leonidas, who had long found his recollections of that same morning offensive enough to ensure he simply buried them, dealt her a cool, unimpressed appraisal. 'Where did you go to shop? Africa?'

'Somewhere rather more convenient. I only drove down the road, but as I turned into the supermarket a car ran into the back of mine. I ended up in hospital with concussion.'

Leonidas studied her in raw disbelief. 'Are you saying that you were involved in a car accident that morning?'

Maribel nodded confirmation.

'Why the hell didn't you phone me?'

'By the time I had recovered my wits enough and had access to a phone you had already left Imogen's house. I took my cue from that fact,' Maribel retorted tightly, her hands clasped together. 'And it cured me of my attachment to you, because I might as well have died for all the interest you had in what had happened to me that day! You didn't even bother to call me.'

Leonidas was still stuck in stunned mode. 'You were hurt…in hospital?'

'Yes, until the following morning.'

The smooth olive planes of his darkly handsome features were taut. Ebony brows pleated with concern, he reached for her hands and drew her towards him. His dark golden eyes were welded to her flushed and defensive face. '*Theos mou,* I am very sorry. If I had known, if I had even suspected that you hadn't returned because something had happened to you, I would have looked for you and I would have been there for you. I thought you had walked out on me.'

Maribel was bewildered. Why would he have thought such a thing? She could not think that he met with rejection of that nature very often. Or was it common for women to behave in such a way after a one-night stand? She didn't want to ask him. She did not want to linger on the subject. She was afraid that her sensitivity might prove all too revealing to a male as shrewd as he was.

Leonidas finally understood why she had said she didn't like him. He was shaken that it had not once occurred to him that she might have had an accident, that there might have been a genuine explanation for her vanishing act. He could not understand why his usual clear-sighted logic should have deserted him that day, or why his reaction had been out of all proportion to the event. But he did recognise the consequences. 'I let you down,' he said gravely. 'I very much regret that, *mali mou*.'

Maribel was taken aback by the sincerity in his lustrous gaze. Her slender fingers smoothed his in a comforting gesture full of all the warmth she would have denied. 'It's all right...you didn't know—'

His wide, sensual mouth twisted. 'It's not all right. I should have enquired. I could have been there with you. But I was arrogant—'

'I know, but you're not about to change,' Maribel told him ruefully. 'Not without an ego transplant.'

Reluctant amusement assailed Leonidas. He lowered his handsome dark head and claimed her soft pink mouth in a passionate onslaught that made the world go into a frantic tailspin around her...

CHAPTER TEN

When the world stopped spinning, Maribel found that Leonidas had propelled her into a bedroom with a soaring ceiling, dimmed lights and a bed the size of a small golf course. 'Is this where you throw orgies?' she asked helplessly.

'You need have no concern on that score. I saw enough of that kind of nonsense growing up with Elora,' Leonidas retorted with derision.

Maribel was transfixed by that frank admission about his late mother. It didn't seem the right moment to tell him that her comment had simply been a bad joke, voiced without thought.

'Aside of the staff, you are the only woman ever to cross the threshold of this room,' Leonidas declared.

Merriment relieved her momentary tension, for she assumed that he was teasing her. 'As if I'd swallow that fairy story!'

'But it is the truth. I have never brought a woman in here before. I have always preferred to keep my bedroom private. It is very rare for me to sleep the whole night through with anyone.'

'You did with me…what was I? An aberration?'

Long brown fingers framed her flushed cheekbones. Her violet-blue eyes subjected him to an unwaveringly direct appraisal. There was no downward and quick upward glance designed to entrap, none of the studied flirtatious moves he was accustomed to receiving from her sex. Instead there was a sincerity he found much more appealing. Slowly a smile began to chase the gravity from his beautifully shaped masculine mouth. 'I would say that addiction would be a more apt description. Here I am back again and that is not like me, *hara mou*. So you must have something unique.'

Something unique? Elias, Maribel filled in ruefully for her own benefit. She could hardly fault him for trying to make his bride feel special on their wedding night. In and out of bed he was too experienced not to know what pleased a woman. He kissed her again with a sweet, intoxicating fervour that soon turned hot and sensual with the dart and plunge of his tongue.

All the tensions of the day found exit in the stormy hunger that took her in a burning tide of desire. Her breath came in short quickened gasps. She stretched up to him, pressing her slim, supple body to his to exchange kiss for kiss with an urgency she could not hold back. He stripped off her dress with impatient hands and lifted her clear of its folds.

Tawny eyes smouldering with purpose, Leonidas stepped back a few inches to get a better look at her. The delicate turquoise lace lingerie revealed rather more than it concealed of her tempting curves and his gaze gleamed with appreciation. 'I like,' he told her sexily against her reddened lips, curving strong hands to her hips to fold her up against his lean, tough, muscular frame.

Even the expensive tailoring of his trousers could not

conceal the hard male heat of his erection. Her breath rasped in her throat. There was an answering tingle of voluptuous response thrumming between her thighs. 'Leonidas…' she gasped under the plundering ravishment of his probing mouth.

'I love your breasts.' He eased the creamy mounds from their lace cups and coaxed the straining rose-tipped crests into almost unbearably tender points. 'The little sounds you make turn me on,' he confided thickly.

Her throat extended as she sucked in oxygen to ease her constricted lungs. But there was no escape from the dark, delirious pleasure that he had taught her to crave with an appetite that could still shock her. Already she was pitched on a high of unquenchable yearning that devoured every sensible thought and destroyed all shame. She was with the man she loved and she liked that very much. He energised her. Insidious heat was whispering through her, every pulse point awakening to the tantalising masculine promise of him, for she knew he would deliver and how.

'Everything about you turns me on, *kardoula mou*,' Leonidas growled. 'You give yourself without pretence.'

He traced the satin wet heat of her beneath the fine material barrier and kneed her legs apart. She shivered violently, every knowing movement of his fingers releasing a cascade of tormenting sensation. She trembled in the high heels she still wore. Every feeling in her body seemed to be concentrated in the tiny sensitive bud at the apex of her thighs. He pushed her unresisting body back against the wall and dropped to his knees to peel off the damp silk. Lean hands cupping the swell of her *derrière*, he brought her to him and indulged in an intimacy that was shockingly new to her.

'No…no,' she mumbled in dismay and dissent.

'Just close your eyes and enjoy,' Leonidas instructed thickly. 'I intend to drive you out of your mind with pleasure.'

The protesting fingers she had dug into his silky black hair lingered to hold him there instead as, all too soon, the sheer seductive delight of what he was doing to her overcame her resistance. She had to lean back against the wall just to stay upright. Her mind was a blank; she was a creature of pure physical response and nothing else mattered. Ripples of wanton pleasure flamed through her in sweet, honeyed waves of rapture. Her blood felt as if it were roaring through her veins. She was gasping, whimpering and out of control when she surged to the point of no return in an explosive climax that shattered her.

Before she had even begun to recover from that erotic onslaught, Leonidas was lifting her to him and bracing her hips back against the wall to tilt her up to receive him. He anchored her knees to his waist. Wildly disconcerted by her position, she looked up at him in confusion. 'Leonidas?'

'All day, every time I looked at you this is where I wanted to be,' he told her with ragged force, plunging his rigid sex deep into the lush, swollen heart of her. 'Inside you, part of you, *hara mou*.'

In that one bold plunge of possession, he deprived her of breath and voice. She was still tender, still descending from the peak of ecstasy, and suddenly he was driving her right back to that same brink for a second time. Extreme sensation returned with blinding force. He slammed into her yielding body with a passion as intense as it was ruthless. The melting, fizzing excitement that seized her was primitive and raw. His fierce passion swept her slowly and steadily to yet another glorious summit where she was overpowered by the exquisite waves of pleasure convulsing her.

'No woman makes me feel as good as you do,' Leonidas whispered in the aftermath.

He carried her over to the bed and settled her down on the cool white linen. He cast off what remained of his clothes and came down beside her. He eased her back into his arms and smoothed her tumbled chestnut hair back from her face. She drank in the aroma of damp musky male that was uniquely him and let her heavy eyes drift closed. She was astonished by the wildness of his love-making, shocked by the level of her response, but content if he was content. She was also overjoyed that he was still holding her.

'You're not going any place, are you?' Maribel felt she had to check after his admission that he preferred not to share a bed.

'Where would I be going?' Leonidas sounded lazily amused.

'Don't want to wake up and find you gone.'

Leonidas remembered emerging from the shower and finding her gone over two years earlier. He had searched the house. He still recalled the sound of the silence, the emptiness that had seemed to echo round him, the hollow sensation inside. The entire episode had seriously spooked him.

'I'll be here,' he confirmed.

'I'm so tired,' she framed drowsily, for now that all her tension had been banished there was nothing left to hold back her bridal exhaustion.

'Happy?' Leonidas prompted.

'Happy,' she mumbled, pressing a sleepy kiss against a smooth brown muscular shoulder.

Leonidas decided that it would be unreasonably cruel to wake her up and tell her about the stag cruise. He would tell her in the morning…some time. He wondered if she would be upset. His arms tightened round her because he really didn't like the idea that any oversight of his might cause her pain.

The third time Maribel woke up the next day, a Greek business channel was playing on the television at the foot of the bed. She flopped back against the pillows with an indolent sigh. It was two in the afternoon. They had breakfasted at seven with Elias and played with him on the shady terrace below the trees. A couple of hours later Leonidas had carried her back to bed. Wakening the second time, she had gone for a shower and he had joined her there. A tender smile curved her reddened mouth. She lifted the television remote and flicked through the channels until she came to a gossipy one about celebrities. She was semi-listening to the entertaining flow of light chatter when Leonidas strolled out of his *en suite* bathroom.

Maribel gave him a rapt appraisal. In a pair of silk boxers and nothing else, he was a magnificent sight.

'Is it worth my while getting dressed again?' Leonidas enquired silkily.

Maribel went pink and gave a little sensual wriggle below the sheet. It would have been true to say that she had not been slow to take advantage of his presence and his amazing stamina.

'I take it that's a no?'

Only the sight of herself in her wedding gown on a television screen could have distracted Maribel at that instant.

She gaped. 'My goodness…doesn't the dress look marvellous?'

'It wasn't the dress, it was you, *kardoula mou*,' Leonidas asserted. 'But I can't believe you're watching rubbish like that.'

'It's more fun than the business news…' Her teasing voice tailed away to a dying whisper because she was listening to the presenter.

"Predictably Leonidas Pallis enjoyed his final days of freedom with a wild stag party on the Torrente yacht, *Diva Queen*."

A party attended by a bunch of naked women, Maribel registered in horror. Although the presenter didn't specifically mention naked women, Maribel's eyes were glued to the screen and she saw a bare-breasted female dancing on deck and another diving off the yacht in what appeared to be her birthday suit…

'Shut up!' she shouted at Leonidas when his attempted vocal intervention threatened to prevent her from hearing the rest of the item. There was a disturbing reference to the existence of more intimate photos which, it was hinted, were unsuitable for general viewing.

'Give me that…' Leonidas lunged for the remote, but Maribel got there first, throwing herself bodily over the top of it. Unfortunately while she won that potential struggle she also accidentally hit the off button.

'You rat!' she exclaimed sickly as she pushed herself back up onto her knees. 'So you don't do orgies? What were you doing on that yacht?'

'Not what you obviously think,' Leonidas countered with a composure that she felt could only add insult to injury. 'Every move I make is sensationalised.'

'A naked woman is a naked woman, and as sensational as things need to get to offend me!' Maribel launched back at him.

'You have to stop believing implicitly in what you see and what you read. Photos and stories can be fabricated.'

'What about the pictures unsuitable for general viewing?'

'If you really want to push this to the limits, I can show you them as well.' Classic profile forbidding and taut, Leonidas hauled on a pair of faded jeans.

'I want to see them.'

That news spelt out in clear defiance of his wishes, which only made her all the more suspicious, Maribel went into the dressing room to rifle cupboards and drawers for clothing. She was acting on automatic pilot. She was trying to build up the strength to deal with the situation, praying that a momentary respite would rescue her brain and her common sense from the feverish emotional grip of anger, fear and pain.

Leonidas wasn't acting as though he had done something wrong. But then, had she ever seen Leonidas act in a guilty manner? And why should he even feel guilty? Why was it only now that she was remembering that he had still not given her an answer to the choice she had given him a month earlier? A platonic marriage in which he would retain his freedom or marital monogamy. Was this his answer? Or just another attention-grabbing paparazzi spread that a sensible woman would rise above and disbelieve as Tilda had suggested? Although Maribel couldn't help feeling that it was rather easier for Tilda to have taken that stance when her own husband was not involved.

Clad in white linen trousers and a fitted white waistcoat

top, Maribel emerged again. Her eyes were a very bright blue against her pallor. Across the depth of the room Leonidas slung her a charged look. The atmosphere was electric with aggressive undertones. He tossed a newspaper down like a statement on the tumbled bed. 'Looking at those pictures is only going to annoy you and give you the wrong impression.'

The tip of her tongue snaked out to moisten her full pink lower lip. 'But I'll always wonder if I don't look at them now.'

'It's a question of trust,' he breathed tautly. 'Who do you believe?'

At that, Maribel lifted her chin. 'I would have believed you if you'd told me about this before I heard about it on television.'

'Was that how you would have preferred our wedding day to begin? With a load of tabloid sleaze aimed at selling a few more papers?'

Discomfiture made Maribel redden and shake her head. 'But when *were* you going to tell me?'

'I foresaw this scenario, *glikia mou*. I have to admit that I wasn't in a hurry.' Golden eyes semi-screened by lush black lashes to gleaming blades challenged her.

'So…er…what are you asking me to believe? That you were kidnapped and forced aboard your friend's yacht where you were subjected to the unwelcome attentions of loose women?'

'Sergio happens to be very into partying right now…he's a friend, a good one. It was a stag do. So, it wasn't to my taste!' Leonidas proclaimed in a raw undertone, lean, strong face set into hard, angular lines of hostility. '*Theos mou*… that ring on my finger doesn't mean that you own me or that you can tell me what I can and can't do!'

'So if I decide to go partying on a yacht with a bunch of half-naked men, that'll be fine with you. You won't ask any awkward questions afterwards. You will fully respect my right to do as I wish. I'm glad we've got that established,' Maribel retorted crisply.

Leonidas froze. Scorching golden eyes locked with hers on a powerful wave of anger. It was like sailing too close to the sun, but she stood her ground. The silence somehow managed to howl around her, laced as it was with intimidating vibrations. Finally, Leonidas spoke. 'That would not be acceptable to me.'

Maribel was not at all surprised by that news. 'And why would that be?'

'You're my wife!' Leonidas grated.

'So you do as you like and I do as you like, too?'

Leonidas refused to take that bait. He surveyed her with dark glittering intensity as if daring her to disagree.

Maribel wondered how they had contrived to roam so far from the main issue and blamed herself for backing away in fear of asking what was undoubtedly the only important question. 'Did you sleep with anyone on that yacht?'

His black brows pleated, the forceful angle of his hard jawline diminishing. 'Of course not.'

Maribel didn't say anything. She was studying the beautiful rug beneath his feet. She felt sick with tension and terror, and dizzy with relief. With a rather jerky nod of acknowledgement she swooped on the paper and went out through the open doors onto the terrace. She was ashamed of how shaken up she was and the reality that her eyes were wet with tears.

Leonidas, who had not been prepared for her to walk out, raked his black hair back off his brow, dissatisfaction seething through him. If he went after her there would be another scene. He had a lifetime of experience at avoiding messy confrontations. All his early memories were of the constant hysterical scenes his late mother had staged with everyone in her life. It was sensible to give Maribel time to calm down. So why, he asked himself in bewilderment, did he want to go after her? Why did the very knowledge that she was alone and unhappy bother him so much? A few minutes later he strode outdoors, only to discover that she was no longer within view.

Maribel made her way through the extensive gardens, plotting a path below the mature trees that shaded her from the sun. The newspaper still felt like a burning brand under her arm. When she reached the beach, she kicked off her shoes and sat down on a rock. The photos weren't quite the shock she had expected. It might have been a party in his honour, but Leonidas looked downright bored. There was one shot of him, lean, bronzed features cold and set, a beautiful skimpily dressed blonde giggling beside him. Maribel knew those facial expressions of his; she knew them so well. She knew he didn't like strangers getting too close and, in much the same way, he disliked women who flung themselves at him. Drunken familiarity really repulsed him. He was a Pallis, an aristocrat born and bred, and he was both fastidious and intolerant of lower standards.

Her throat was thick with the tears she was choking back. She flung the newspaper down. In one sense she was the one with the problem, not him. She was insecure, but she was only getting what she had asked for. He had married her, hadn't he? But he had only put that ring on her finger for Elias' sake. How safe and secure had she expected to feel in those circumstances? He had had a perfect right to enjoy a stag do within reasonable boundaries and to expect his new wife not to make a big deal out of it. He was also entitled to expect her to trust him to some extent at least. How long would their marriage last if she continually made unjust accusations? She was jealous and insecure, but he should not have to pay the price for that. Those feelings, Maribel reckoned painfully, were the price of marrying a guy who didn't love her.

Footsteps crunched across the sand. A long shadow fell over her as Leonidas drew level with her.

Maribel stood up. 'I'm sorry,' she whispered jaggedly. 'I wasn't giving you a fair hearing.'

Leonidas expelled his breath on a hiss and pulled her into his arms. He rested his brow on the top of her head. 'On my honour, I swear that nothing happened. Do you believe me?'

'Yes.' Maribel gulped. 'You look awfully fed up in those photos.'

'That was the lifestyle I grew up with and it wrecked the family I might have had. Drugs destroyed my mother, Elora's health and infidelity ruined her relationships. My older sister followed in her footsteps,' he acknowledged grimly. 'Elora conceived me by one man on the same day that she married another. By the time the truth came out, my real father was dead and the man I thought was my father turned his back on me. How's that for screwing up? But I have always wanted and needed more from my life.'

'I know.' She found his hands and squeezed them. When she thought of how hard she tried to protect Elias from hurt she was filled with angry regret on Leonidas' behalf. He had been forced to learn hard lessons at too young an age. 'You're strong. But I need to trust you. I know that.'

'It's my fault that you couldn't.' Leonidas regarded her with level dark golden eyes. 'I should have told you before the wedding but I was too proud—I don't want anyone else but you, *hara mou*.'

Maribel was unprepared for that admission. She swallowed hard and closed her eyes tight. Suddenly her heart felt light and the shadows were lifting from her. He was telling her so much more than he was saying. He really did want their marriage to work. He was prepared to make the effort. She thought back to her blind foolishness the day before, when she had informed him that she no longer loved him, and she almost groaned out loud. How short-sighted she had been! It was time that she ditched some of her pride and defensiveness.

'With a wife who wakes me up during the night to have her wicked way with me, where would I get the energy?' Leonidas murmured teasingly.

Maribel flushed to the roots of her hair. 'I didn't mean to waken you. It was dark—I wasn't sure where I was—'

'Excuses…excuses.' Leonidas treated her to a smouldering visual appraisal that made her tummy turn a somersault. 'But tonight it'll be my turn, *mali mou*.'

Elias was fast asleep on his stomach with his bottom in the air. Maribel gently rearranged him into a cooler position. Exhausted, he did not even stir. Her son's days were packed with adventure, for the Pallis estate was a wonderful playground for a child as active as he was. From dawn to dusk Elias was on the go, playing in the pool with his parents or just running round with Mouse, who was now travelling on a swanky pet passport.

Maribel dressed up for dinner. It was a special evening

because it was to be their last night on Zelos for a while. For the past week, Leonidas had been flying in and out on business at all hours in an effort to extend their stay on the island for as long as possible. He seemed as reluctant as she was to leave, as they'd had a magical honeymoon.

Certainly, Maribel conceded, she had never dreamt that she might find such happiness so quickly with Leonidas. She had first seen him discard his famous reserve with his son, but with every week that had passed since she'd become his wife he seemed to relax his guard more with her. She noticed the little things the most. If he had to work in his office for a while, he would come looking for her afterwards. He wakened her to have breakfast with him at an ungodly hour because he clearly wanted her company. He liked her to see him right out to the helipad and he really loved it if she waited up for him when he was late home.

And she had begun to appreciate that all his life he had been horribly starved of genuine affection and any form of conventional home-based routine. Things she took for granted, like sitting down to eat a meal with Elias, he set a high value on. He enjoyed the simple pleasures—a walk with Elias through the citrus orchards to the shore, where their son would toddle in the waves and shout in delight when he got wet. Leonidas liked the little rituals of family life that she had naïvely feared he would consider boring, restrictive or outdated. What he had never had he wanted Elias to have, and he adored his son. Nobody watching Leonidas smile as Elias raced to greet him could have doubted that.

Seeing Greece through his eyes, she had fallen more in love with it than ever, after he had taken her off the tourist track on his yacht. In his company she had explored some fascinating ancient archaeological sites. He had shown her his favourite places, some hauntingly beautiful and almost all deserted. He had also taught her that, if the food was good, he was happier eating at a rickety table in a tiny taverna in a hillside village than he was in an exclusive restaurant. They had picnicked and swum in unspoilt coves that could only be reached from the sea. Above all, he prized his privacy and even though he was almost always recognised his countrymen awarded him that space.

Maribel had worked hard at losing the habit of making unfavourable comparisons between herself and Imogen. She had accepted that it was stupid to continually torment herself with such ego-zapping thoughts and she had concentrated instead on recognising what she did have with Leonidas. And what she had, she reflected dreamily, was a lot more than she had ever dared to hope for. He was her every fantasy come true in the bedroom. He was highly intelligent, great, cool company and very witty. She was learning how dependable he was, how straightforward he could be once the barriers came down. He could also be wonderfully gentle and considerate.

A slim, stylish figure clad in a strappy emerald-green sundress, Maribel strolled out onto the terrace that overlooked the bay. It was gloriously cool below the spreading canopy of the walnut trees. Only a few minutes later, Leonidas came out to join her. His mobile phone was ringing, but he paused only to switch it off and set it aside. The staff knew better than to interrupt him with anything less than an emergency. Her dark blue eyes locked to his lean, darkly handsome face. His presence always created a buzz and, true to form, he looked amazing in a cream open-necked shirt and jeans.

'We've been together one calendar month, *hara mou*,' Leonidas filled two flutes with champagne and handed a jewel box to her. 'That calls for a celebration.'

Taken aback, Maribel lifted the lid. Her breath caught in her throat at the beauty of the diamond bracelet with the initials MP picked out in sapphires. She now knew how much he enjoyed giving her presents and she no longer scolded him for it.

'It's really gorgeous, Leonidas. Put it on for me,' she urged. 'Now I feel bad because I've got nothing to give you!'

Leonidas looked down at his wife with sensual dark eyes. 'Don't worry. I'll come up with something that doesn't cost you anything but lost sleep.'

Maribel blushed and grinned and extended her wrist until the light filtering through the trees glittered over the jewels. 'Thank you,' she told him.

He passed her a champagne flute. 'Before I forget to mention it, your cousin Amanda phoned to ask us to a dinner party in London. I was surprised she didn't ring you.'

Maribel wasn't surprised. Amanda was as ruthless at making use of influential contacts as her mother was and would have deliberately contacted Leonidas in preference to her cousin. 'I think I'll make a polite excuse,' she said uncomfortably. 'My relatives are going through a bit of an adjustment period just now. It's probably best if I let them have some time to get used to the fact that you're my husband.'

Leonidas quirked an eloquent black brow. 'What on earth are you talking about? Why should they need time?'

Maribel winced. 'The Strattons were rather like the spectres at our wedding feast,' she admitted ruefully. 'I'm afraid my aunt was initially very upset when she realised that you were Elias' father—'

His brilliant dark eyes flashed gold.' How was that her business?'

'I know it's a long time ago, but you and Imogen were once an item.' It was a reluctant reminder, for Maribel was already wishing she had chosen to be less frank on the subject. The habit she had recently developed of telling Leonidas everything had gone deeper than she appreciated.

'No, we weren't.'

'Possibly not on your terms.' Maribel was performing a mental dance to choose the right words to explain how her relatives felt. 'Had you had a child with anyone but me and married that person, it wouldn't have bothered them. But when it's me, they can't seem to stop thinking that I somehow poached on Imogen's preserves.'

Leonidas frowned. 'But I didn't date Imogen.'

Maribel stared fixedly at him. 'Maybe you didn't call it dating, but you were involved with her for a while—'

'Sexually?' Leonidas cut in. 'No, I wasn't.'

Gobsmacked by a statement that turned years of conviction upside down, Maribel shook her head as though to clear it. 'But that's not possible. I mean, Imogen herself *said*—I mean, she talked as if—'

'I don't care what she said, *hara mou*. It didn't happen. *Ever*,' Leonidas said dryly.

'Oh, my goodness.' Maribel gazed wide-eyed back at him. 'She let everyone think that you had been lovers.'

'No doubt she liked the attention it brought her, but she didn't appeal to me on that level.'

Maribel nodded like a marionette, because she could scarcely get her mind round the obvious fact that

Leonidas had been more attracted to her than he had ever been to her beautiful cousin. 'But...but *why* weren't you attracted to her?'

'She was good fun, but she was also neurotic and superficial.' A frown line pleated his fine brows as if he was engaging in deeper thought as well. 'To be blunt, I knew she wanted me. I assumed that that was why you said you weren't interested when I kissed you—'

Maribel was bemused and momentarily lost. 'Kissed... me...*when*?'

Leonidas shrugged. 'When I was a student staying in Imogen's house.'

'You mean that was a genuine pass...not just some sort of a bad-boy joke?' Maribel stammered, her mind leaping back almost seven years.

'Is that what you thought?' Leonidas gave her a wry look. 'You pushed me away and it was the right thing to do. Back then, I would definitely have screwed up with you. I didn't know what was going on inside my own head. Imogen would have got in the way as well. I realised even then that if she couldn't have me, she didn't want you to have me either.'

Maribel was hanging on his every word. Discovering that Leonidas had been attracted to her that far back, at the same time as she learnt that he had never wanted Imogen, transformed Maribel's view of her entire relationship with him. Only now could she see that there had been a definite history between them before they had first shared a bed.

'Remember the night I told you about my sister? That was when I realised that I wanted you because, afterwards, I didn't know what I had been doing there in your room talking about all that personal stuff—'

'Drunk and in Greek,' Maribel slotted in helplessly.

'But I'd never done anything like that before with a woman.' Leonidas mimicked an uneasy masculine shiver. 'It…it disturbed me that you had this mental pull on me that I couldn't explain. It was too deep and I wasn't ready for anything deep at the time.'

'I know,' Maribel said feelingly, but the joy was rising steadily inside her, as she would never again have to feel as though she was second-best to her cousin. Imogen had lied about the level of her involvement with Leonidas—which didn't really surprise Maribel when she thought about it.

'Imogen told me you cared about me and it was supposed to be a joke,' Leonidas confided, dark golden eyes resting tautly on her. 'But I liked the idea and it drew me to you even more, *kardoula mou.*'

Her cheeks were a warm peach. Unsure what to say, she breathed, 'But you were upset after Imogen's funeral.'

'At the waste of her life, yes. It took me back to when my mother and my sister died. I tried to help Imogen and I failed,' Leonidas murmured gravely. 'When she abandoned rehab, I turned my back on her because I refused to watch her die.'

'You did your best and you weren't the only one. Nothing worked,' Maribel breathed with tears glistening in her blue eyes.

'But you did watch over her and support her long after other people gave up on her. That level of loyalty and love is very rare. I recognised that, even if her family didn't. When I saw you again at the funeral, nothing would have stopped me seeking you out.'

'What are you saying?' Maribel whispered.

'That if it hadn't been for your cousin, we would never

have met. But once I met you, no other woman really had a chance with me because there was so much in you that I admired.'

'Even if you weren't quite ready for all that stuff you admired in me?' Mirabel prompted unevenly.

'Even then. You were clever and gutsy and not at all impressed by me or my money. Our first night together was very special——'

'Special? All you did was ask for breakfast afterwards.'

Leonidas spread lean brown hands in an expressive gesture of reproach at that judgement. '*Theos mou*, I didn't know what to say. I didn't even appreciate that anything needed to be said in that moment. I suppose I was out of my comfort zone. All I knew was that I was in a wonderful mood. I felt so natural with you. I was devastated when I came out of the shower and found an empty house!' Leonidas admitted in a raw undertone. 'No note, no phone call—nothing!'

Maribel stared at him in horror. 'D-devastated?'

'And then very angry with you because you'd walked out on me. I took it as a rejection and I wouldn't let myself think about it because it *hurt*…' That last word cost him such an effort to get out that it was almost whispered.

Tears were trickling down Maribel's cheeks. 'Oh, Leonidas…'

He removed the champagne glass from her fingers and set it aside so that he could pull her close and comfort her with a tenderness that made her cling to him for a few minutes. 'Of course, I went to the memorial service looking for you without even admitting that to myself. And then when I did, telling myself that it was only because we'd had great sex.'

Maribel sniffed and stole a hanky off him. 'If only I hadn't had that accident,' she sighed.

'But we're together now and I will never let you go.' He admitted how nervous he had been on their wedding day over the bad publicity concerning the stag cruise. Maribel, who had thought he didn't have nerves, was entranced by the idea that she had that much influence over him. When he confided that they had ended up on Zelos, rather than in Italy, because he had been afraid that she might try to leave him she broke down into helpless giggles.

Leonidas slid lean fingers into her chestnut hair and tipped her head back to scan her with steady dark golden eyes of appreciation. 'I know, it's hilarious. Loving you does fill my head with freaky thoughts and fears.'

Maribel stopped laughing. 'Loving me?' she parroted.

'I really, really do love you,' Leonidas declared huskily.

Maribel gazed up at him in wonderment.

'I fought it hard. But there was no escaping it,' Leonidas said ruefully. 'You put me through an emotional wringer—telling me what a lousy father I would be and how irresponsible I was. That was a massive shock to my system and a challenge. I went haywire for a few weeks. Why do you think I engineered that story in the newspaper to expose our relationship? I was seriously jealous of your boyfriend.'

'Sloan? You were jealous? We only had one date.' But Maribel was thrilled that he had been roused to jealousy, for it made her feel wonderfully like a *femme fatale*. 'You truly love me?'

'Didn't I marry you without demanding DNA tests for Elias? Or the safety net of a pre-nup? Didn't you appreciate how much I had to trust and value you to do that?' Leonidas gave her an appreciative appraisal, his dark eyes rich and mellow as honey. 'And why do you think I let you blackmail me into marrying you?'

'To get me back in bed?'

'There is that angle,' Leonidas was honest enough to acknowledge, a wolfish grin curving his handsome mouth. 'But it is what I wanted too, so I let myself be blackmailed. I would have got around to asking you eventually, but you got in first. That allowed me to save face.'

Maribel couldn't stop smiling and only just remembered that she had something to say too. 'I was lying when I said I got over you. I've been in love with you for so long, you're like a fixture in my heart.'

Leonidas had tensed. 'You lied? You *mean*—'

'Now don't take it so personally. A girl's got to do what a girl's got to do sometimes and, after all that stuff you talked about our marriage being a business arrangement and demanding sex up front, you didn't really deserve a confession of true love.' Maribel eased caressing hands of distraction beneath his shirt. 'But I do love you very very much.'

'Is that the truth?'

Maribel was touched by his uncertainty. 'Yes. I love you.'

'Your penance for withholding that information is that you don't get to eat. We're going to bed, *agape mou*.' Leonidas took her ripe lips in a single hungry kiss of heated intent that left her breathless and with weak knees. Then he peeled her off him again and closed a hand over hers to urge her back indoors. She had absolutely no quarrel with his plan of action.

A long time later, Maribel lying comfortably wrapped in his arms and hand-fed with appetising nibbles and sips of wine to conserve her strength, Leonidas confessed that he was sad that he had missed out on the whole experience of her being pregnant, not to mention the first months of their son's life.

'We could have another baby,' Maribel conceded.

'I'd like that, *agape mou.*'

'But not just yet.' Maribel ran a possessive hand over his lean muscular torso and buried her cheek there. 'When I'm pregnant, I spend most of the time wanting to sleep.'

'Not just yet,' Leonidas agreed with a ragged edge to his dark drawl.

Two years later, Sofia Pallis was born.

Mirabel's second pregnancy suffered from none of the anxieties that had burdened the first. With staff to help at every turn, she retained her usual energy right up until the last few weeks. Leonidas took a great interest in every development. It brought them even closer and she really enjoyed carrying her daughter. When her due date came close, Leonidas wouldn't go abroad in case she went into labour early and he stayed with her when Sofia was born. His delight in their daughter was the equal of her own.

Sofia took after both her parents. She inherited her father's lustrous dark brown eyes and her mother's delicate features. Now three-and-a-half years old, Elias was fascinated with his baby sister, but rather disappointed that she couldn't even sit up to play with him.

'She's so little,' Elias lamented with all the drama of a Pallis.

'Sofia will grow,' his mother consoled him.

'She yells a lot.'

'You did too when you were a baby.' Having settled her

infant daughter for the night in the nursery next door, Maribel tugged back the duvet to encourage Elias into bed. He climbed in with a truck tucked under one arm.

Leonidas appeared in the doorway while Maribel was reading a bedtime story. She smiled across the room at him, her heart in her eyes, for he had made her extraordinarily happy and she was not a woman to take that good fortune for granted. When the story was finished, Leonidas walked across the room and opened the door of the built in closet. Mouse unfolded his shaggy limbs and got up to greet him with innocent enthusiasm.

'Dad!' Elias wailed in protest.

'Mouse sleeps downstairs.'

'You're getting so tough,' Maribel told her husband outside their son's bedroom door.

Leonidas laughed softly. 'But Elias was clever hiding the dog like that.'

'No, he was sneaky and so I shall tell him tomorrow when I have the time to explain the difference,' Maribel told him staunchly.

'Who says cunning is always wrong?' Leonidas studied her with smouldering dark golden eyes of appreciation. 'Didn't I take advantage of you on the night that Elias was conceived? There you were all weepy and emotional and lonely and I made the most of the occasion.'

Maribel was shaken by that take on the past. 'I never thought of it that way before.'

'And as long as I live I won't regret it, *agape mou*.' Leonidas breathed with raw sincerity. 'I have you and Elias and Sofia and you are the most precious elements in my world. I cannot imagine my life without you.'

It was the same for Maribel. Her heart was full to overflowing at that instant. He told her how much he loved her and she responded with the same fervour, for they both knew that the strong bonds they shared were very precious. Once Leonidas and Maribel had moved out of sight and hearing, Mouse slunk back upstairs and back into Elias' room again.

THE ROYAL HOUSE OF NIROLI

*...International affairs, seduction
and passion guaranteed*

Volume 5 – November 2007
Expecting His Royal Baby by Susan Stephens

Volume 6 – December 2007
The Prince's Forbidden Virgin by Robyn Donald

Volume 7 – January 2008
Bride by Royal Appointment by Raye Morgan

Volume 8 – February 2008
A Royal Bride at the Sheikh's Command by Penny Jordan

8 volumes in all to collect!

Celebrate 100 years of pure reading pleasure with Mills & Boon®

To mark our centenary, each month we're publishing a special 100th Birthday Edition. These celebratory editions are packed with extra features and include a FREE bonus story.

Now that's worth celebrating!

4th January 2008

The Vanishing Viscountess by Diane Gaston
With FREE story The Mysterious Miss M
This award-winning tale of the Regency Underworld launched Diane Gaston's writing career.

1st February 2008

Cattle Rancher, Secret Son by Margaret Way
With FREE story His Heiress Wife
Margaret Way excels at rugged Outback heroes…

15th February 2008

Raintree: Inferno by Linda Howard
With FREE story Loving Evangeline
A double dose of Linda Howard's heady mix of passion and adventure.

Don't miss out! From February you'll have the chance to enter our fabulous monthly prize draw. See special 100th Birthday Editions for details.

www.millsandboon.co.uk

FREE

4 BOOKS AND A SURPRISE GIFT!

We would like to take this opportunity to thank you for reading this Mills & Boon® book by offering you the chance to take FOUR more specially selected titles from the Modern™ series absolutely FREE! We're also making this offer to introduce you to the benefits of the Mills & Boon® Reader Service™—

- ★ **FREE home delivery**
- ★ **FREE gifts and competitions**
- ★ **FREE monthly Newsletter**
- ★ **Books available before they're in the shops**
- ★ **Exclusive Reader Service offers**

Accepting these FREE books and gift places you under no obligation to buy; you may cancel at any time, even after receiving your free shipment. Simply complete your details below and return the entire page to the address below. You don't even need a stamp!

YES! Please send me 4 free Modern books and a surprise gift. I understand that unless you hear from me, I will receive 6 superb new titles every month for just £2.89 each, postage and packing free. I am under no obligation to purchase any books and may cancel my subscription at any time. The free books and gift will be mine to keep in any case.

P8ZEE

Ms/Mrs/Miss/Mr..Initials ....

BLOCK CAPITALS PLEASE

Surname ....

Address ....

....

....Postcode ....

Send this whole page to:
The Reader Service, FREEPOST CN81, Croydon, CR9 3WZ